ESCAPING WITH YOU

WRIGHT HEROES OF MAINE, A PREQUEL
BOOK 0

ROBIN PATCHEN

JDO PUBLISHING

Paperback: 978-1-950029-50-1

Large Print: 978-1-950029-51-8

Hard Cover: 978-1-950029-52-5

Cover design by Lynnette Bonner

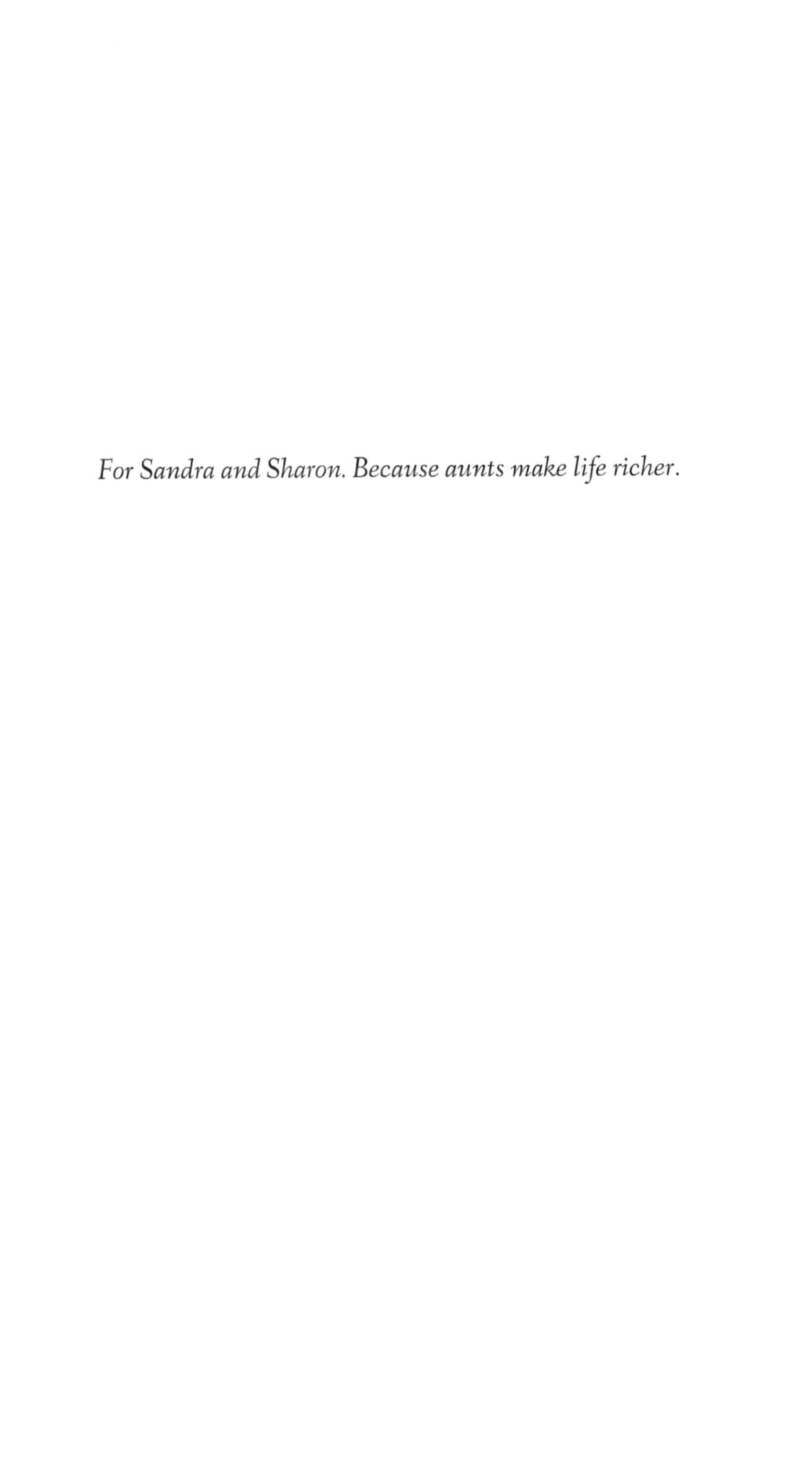

For Sandra and Sharon. Because aunts make life richer.

CHAPTER ONE

Even before the gunshots, Logan Webb was having a bad day.

An hour earlier, he'd stared past the round tables and chairs —and all the people—in the retreat center's common room, and watched Darcy, wishing he had the courage to talk to her. And a little thankful he didn't.

The sooner she left, the sooner he could quit thinking about all the could-have-beens.

It was only midafternoon, but he was exhausted as he worked behind the buffet table in the brand-new retreat center on the outskirts of Shadow Cove, Maine. His tenth high school reunion weekend was almost over, and it couldn't end soon enough. Not that he hadn't enjoyed having old friends in town, but he'd spent most of the weekend in the kitchen. His restaurant had catered the formal ball the night before and Friday evening's family dinner. Today's seminar and book signing—featuring the only celebrity their little town boasted, even if she spent most of her time in New York these days—was the final event.

"How'd it work out?"

Logan tore his gaze away from Darcy to find his friend and mentor, Miles O'Neil, approaching from the office. Logan grabbed the platter of leftover sandwiches, pretending he hadn't been staring. "No problems at all."

Miles, manager of Retreats at Hidden Grove, grabbed an armful of condiments and followed Logan into the kitchen. "Where do you want these?"

Logan nodded to a plastic bin, and Miles shifted the bottles of ketchup, mustard, and mayo inside.

"You had everything you needed?"

"Yup, it's perfect." Logan glanced around at the commercial kitchen he'd enjoyed all weekend, with its shiny appliances and oversize cooktops. A far cry from the too-small, too-old kitchen in his restaurant in town.

Miles closed the lid on the condiment container. "If you think of anything we need, let me know. Sam wants this place to be the new go-to event center in Maine."

"He's a good guy, Sam Wright?" Logan barely knew the man. Sam had moved to Shadow Cove a few years before, and Logan had talked to him a couple of times at church and when he came into the restaurant.

"Great guy. I think he planned to sell this property, but the way the market's turned..." Miles grinned. "The job works out well for me. After Linny's death, I needed..." His voice faded, and he collected serving utensils, shifting them nearer the empty bins. "You did well. After this, you'll be our recommended caterer."

"Okay." Logan tried to hide his relief. He'd invested thousands in the catering equipment and van. It was a risk, and if it failed, he could destroy the business his father had built. Landing the Hidden Grove account would go a long way toward making it successful.

"Sam was impressed with you," Miles said. "He's someone

you want on your side." Miles propped a hip against one of the stainless-steel prep tables.

"I'm not looking to win friends and influence people," Logan said. "I just want to feed my family." His mother and siblings were his responsibility now that Dad was gone. Everything he'd done since the funeral, he'd done for them.

"There are the Sam Wrights in the world," Miles said. "And the MJ Partingtons." Miles glanced through the serving window between the kitchen and the event space, where the bestselling author was holding court, her niece beside her.

Logan didn't follow his gaze. He needed to stop looking at Darcy. He needed to stop wishing everything had been different.

Miles continued. "And then there are guys like you and me. Just regular folks making a living."

"Trying to, anyway." The reminder was good for Logan today. Darcy Partington was out of his league and always had been. He needed to quit hoping something might change.

He emptied the commercial dishwasher, separating the things he'd brought from those owned by the retreat center.

Laughter erupted from the ballroom, where MJ was still entertaining fans while Darcy tapped at her phone as if she could conjure cell phone service by sheer will. Or maybe she was just avoiding meeting Logan's eyes. Not that he could blame her. He'd been avoiding meeting hers for three hours.

Thank God, Darcy hadn't gone to high school with him or he'd have had to avoid her all weekend.

"She sure knows how to work a room."

Miles meant MJ, of course. The celebrity.

"You two are about the same age, right?" Logan asked. "Did you know her in school?"

"Nah. Your dad and I were a few years older than Mary Jane."

Mary Jane. Huh. Logan had only known her as Aunt MJ, who always had Country Time Lemonade and store-bought cookies, who came home from work in business suits and promptly changed into ratty shorts and T-shirts and plopped on the deck to enjoy a glass of wine with Darcy's mom.

"Can I help?" Miles asked.

Logan had to tear his eyes away from the woman in the other room. "I got it. Thanks. And for the opportunity. It means a lot."

"Anything for you, kid."

Miles had called him *kid* as long as Logan could remember, since way back when Dad was alive and life was about crab gigging and racing his best friend down the beach.

When they were little, Darcy had won those races. And then Logan hit a growth spurt and...

And he had to stop thinking about her.

"Don't work too hard," Miles said. "God's your family's provider, not you."

Sure. Of course. But God used Logan to do it. And if he screwed it up...

A shadow crossed Miles's features, a tiny hint of what must be going on inside.

Logan asked, "How are you doing?"

"It's hard. The anniversary's coming up."

Miles had lost his wife to cancer when Logan was in high school. Miles's daughter had passed away almost a year ago.

Logan remembered thinking the first year after Dad's death would be the hardest, and then it would get easier. And it did, to a degree. But...not to the degree he'd expected. Even now, almost a decade later, the grief rose sometimes.

He couldn't imagine what Miles was going through. Bad enough Linny had died, but to overdose so long after she'd kicked the drugs. Or at least Miles thought she had.

Miles had been there for Logan when Dad died. He tried to be there for Miles. But what was there to say? To do?

Miles clamped him on the shoulder. "Lock up when everybody's gone, would you?"

"No problem."

After the older man headed for the back door and let himself out, Logan resumed cleaning the kitchen and packing up. This would go faster if Jewel would help, but she spent as much time visiting as she did working. He glanced back into the dining room to see where his sister had gone. No sign of her.

Darcy swung a set of keys from her finger. She'd pressed on a patient smile. Her natural blond hair fell in soft waves around her face. She was all business in black slacks, a dark gray button-down, and black heels that added at least three inches to her five-five frame. She was slender but not as thin as she'd been in college. He liked the curves.

"She looks great." His sister had slipped in while his focus had been on Darcy. Again.

"Who?"

"You're as transparent as plastic wrap." Jewel rolled her eyes, reminding him of the teenager she'd been not that long ago. "Darcy said they're going straight to the airport. Your window is closing."

He needed it to close, slam shut, and lock tight. He'd given up a lot of things—his college degree, his dreams for a career.

In retrospect, those things hadn't been sacrifices. He was where he was supposed to be, doing what he was supposed to do. Aside from the pressure of supporting his family, he loved his life.

He only had one regret, and the sooner she returned to New York, the better.

He pressed the top onto a plastic bin. One of the pots inside was askew, preventing the lid from catching. He yanked it off, adjusted the contents, and tried again.

"Don't blame the pans," Jewel said. "It's not their fault you're a coward."

He held the bin out to her. "Why don't you make yourself useful for a change?"

She ignored—or more likely, enjoyed—his irritation. "I can finish up here." She tilted her head to the side, her expression morphing from amusement to something else—something tender. "As much as you've tried not to look at Darcy, she's been trying not to look at you. Just go talk to her."

"I don't need advice from a toddler."

His sister stuck out her tongue, and he grinned as he grabbed the last few things off the buffet table.

Was Jewel right? Had Darcy been watching him? More than once he'd thought he felt her gaze. Somehow, they'd managed to get through the entire three-hour event without coming within fifteen feet of each other. He'd been busy preparing, serving, and now cleaning up.

When Darcy hadn't been tending to her aunt and selling books, she was on her phone, looking frustrated. Apparently, she'd forgotten how to survive without instant access to everything.

One more good reason for their breakup. He was perfectly at home in these woods, miles from civilization.

Darcy's idea of roughing it was a Lyft instead of a limo.

In the kitchen, Logan stacked clean dishes—fresh out of the brand-new commercial dishwasher he was trying not to covet—into the cabinets.

Jewel returned from carrying the bin to the van. "A bunch of your friends are headed to The Salty Frog. Why don't you let me finish up here? You can get a ride with them, and I'll drive the van back."

He shot her a quick smile. "I'm not up for any more socializing this weekend."

"What socializing? You worked nonstop. I can handle it."

"I didn't say you couldn't." Even if he thought so. Jewel was just a kid—barely twenty-three. He wasn't about to risk messing up the opportunity of Hidden Grove's catering contract so he could go have a beer with his buddies. "I'll just—"

"Live like a cloistered monk because you don't trust me. At least one of us should have a life." She yanked off her apron and tossed it in a bin of sandwich rolls. "See you later."

They'd driven up there together, so... "How are you—?"

"Your friends will drive me." She spoke over her shoulder as she walked out.

He stifled a growl. His little sister wasn't so little anymore. He didn't miss the way guys looked at her, and he didn't like it.

He was tempted to go out and have a chat with his old friends, reminding them of the bro code—no hitting on sisters. But, as Mom kept telling him, Jewel was an adult and could make her own decisions.

When it came to Jewel, Logan wanted to put quotation marks around that word—*adult*.

In the other room, Jewel stopped to speak to Darcy. They shared a brief hug. And then both women glanced his way.

He got back to work. Who cared if they talked to each other? Didn't matter to him.

He finished up, leaving the kitchen as nice as he'd found it, while trying not to notice as the door in the other room opened and closed, over and over, until finally, the voices faded completely, leaving the building empty.

He risked a glance. Yup. Darcy was gone. Fair turnabout, considering the last time they parted, he'd done the leaving. And that had been excruciating.

It didn't hurt any less today.

CHAPTER TWO

————————

Darcy Partington had spent every summer of her childhood at her aunt's house in Shadow Cove, and she'd loved it. In fact, the cottage overlooking the Atlantic had felt more like home to her than her family's oversize Connecticut house ever did.

But after Logan dumped her, she'd only returned to Shadow Cove once—for his father's funeral.

She wouldn't have come this weekend if MJ hadn't insisted. Since Darcy's aunt was the publisher's biggest seller—and Darcy, her publicist—she hadn't had a choice.

She'd thought Logan would keep his distance. It hadn't occurred to her that he'd cater the event. Not only had he kept his dad's business afloat, he was expanding. She was glad for his success.

She was successful too. They'd once planned a life together, but it seemed they were both doing just fine on their own.

She glared at the low-hanging clouds as she and MJ headed toward the rental car. It was August, for crying out loud. The forecast had predicted mideighties in Manhattan today, but they were a long way from New York. It couldn't be more than seventy here, and with the humidity and the breeze, it felt colder than that. She'd check the temperature if her stupid phone had service.

Yeah, lack of connectivity. And the weather. Those were the problems.

Not the man she'd tried hard to pretend didn't exist.

Fine. She'd noticed how good Logan looked. He wore his blond hair shorter now. The facial hair was new. She'd half expected him to have a paunch—weren't cooks supposed to get fat? No joy there.

"Logan looked better than ever." MJ had read Darcy's mind, as usual.

Darcy stowed the suitcase of books and promotional materials in the trunk and slammed it shut. "I didn't notice."

"Riiight."

After sharing a meal with strangers, giving an hour-long speech, and then signing books for another hour, the sixty-one-year-old should look haggard. But no, Darcy's aunt looked as fresh as she had that morning, not a single silver hair out of place. She wore her standard book-signing outfit—a dark red suit jacket with matching slacks paired with a light gray camisole. Today, MJ had chosen silver dangle earrings shaped like lobsters —to remind people she was a local. "I can't believe you didn't even say hello." She climbed into the passenger side, and Darcy settled in to drive.

She didn't bother trying to bring up the map back to the airport in Portland. Once they hit the highway, she'd have service again. They just had to make it out of the woods.

As she headed back toward civilization, away from the only building for miles around, the road seemed narrower than it had on her way in. There were no sidewalks, no shoulders on either side, just two lanes separated from wilderness by nothing but a skinny strip of gravel.

No houses, no businesses, not even a lonely gas station.

"Why didn't you?" MJ asked.

"Why didn't I what?" Not that Darcy didn't know what her aunt was talking about. Or *who*, to be more precise.

"Don't play games."

"It's over between Logan and me. What would've been the point in talking to him?"

"To find out how he is. You used to love him, after all."

Yeah, well... He'd started it, the avoiding-each-other thing.

Darcy was doing fine without Logan. Better than fine. She rubbed shoulders with New York's publishing elite and their clients—politicians, entrepreneurs, people at the height of their careers. She had everything she'd ever wanted.

MJ tried again to draw her into conversation about her ex, but Darcy had learned the gentle art of distraction.

"Any update on Xavier and the lawsuit?" MJ's former editor was suing the publisher, claiming he'd been wrongfully terminated.

"You didn't hear?"

"I never hear anything." Darcy had better things to do than stand around the proverbial water cooler and gossip.

"The suit was thrown out."

MJ's thoughtful tone surprised Darcy. "That's good news, right?"

"He was a good editor."

"Who threatened you."

MJ brushed off the words with a flick of her wrist. "Why he thought I had anything to do with his getting fired, I have no idea."

Darcy had heard a rumor about that, but she hadn't shared it with MJ, feeling trapped between loyalty to her aunt and loyalty to her employer. If she thought it would help anything—

not add fuel to a fire that was finally petering out—she would tell her.

"I was always happy with his work. The guy I have now…" MJ enumerated all the differences between her former editor and her current one. All Darcy had to do was nod at the right times, and MJ wouldn't notice she was barely paying attention.

She'd been polite to a hundred strangers while managing MJ's book sales—and that was on top of all the energy that had gone into *not* talking to Logan. Darcy was exhausted.

They'd be at the airport in an hour. God willing, she'd be back at her apartment by midnight.

Tomorrow, she'd work from home. No makeup, no putting on slacks, no torturous heels. Just a pot of coffee and her laptop.

She was angling around a sharp corner when a boom sounded.

The car jerked into a skid.

She braked and yanked the wheel in the opposite direction, barely staying on the road. "It's a blowout. I'll—"

"Don't stop!" Her aunt's shout was filled with terror.

"What? We have to—"

Another boom reverberated. This time, the car didn't jerk.

Not a blowout.

But what…?

A gunshot?

Before her mind caught up with her instincts, Darcy pressed the gas pedal, fighting the steering wheel to keep the car with its ruined tire on the road.

And then a man jogged onto the road not twenty-five yards in front of them. He wore all black, from his boots to a mask that covered everything but his eyes.

He aimed a rifle at them.

She slammed on the brakes.

"Go, go!" MJ sounded frantic, panicked.

Darcy jammed the car into reverse. She maneuvered backward, looking over her shoulder and going as fast as she dared. They were rounding a bend when another boom sounded.

The rear passenger window exploded.

MJ screamed.

Darcy jerked the wheel too hard.

The car veered a few yards into the woods and smashed into a tree.

No, no, no!

She yanked the gear into drive. The car rocked forward—and back again—the sound of metal against metal grating, deafening. She jammed her foot on the gas, but they were stuck.

"Come on!" MJ opened her door, jumped out, and bolted into the woods. Within seconds, she disappeared.

Darcy climbed over the console and followed. Crouching low, she darted around bushes and trees into the forest. Just a few feet in, she reached a steep drop-off and slowed.

A gunshot sounded, and she dropped, rolled to her stomach, and slid to the bottom.

CHAPTER THREE

The first rifle shot had the little hairs on Logan's neck prickling.

It wasn't hunting season, but someone could be up here shooting at targets. He and his father had come to the cabin in these woods for target practice many times when Logan was a kid.

He set the crate of leftovers into the van and returned to the kitchen door to finish up. He was pushing buttons on the electronic lock when the second shot came.

He turned toward the noise. Thanks to the echo, it was hard to be sure, but it sounded like it came not from the acres of forest behind the building but from the opposite side, where the road led to the highway a few miles away.

His gut clenched.

The woods around the event center should be off-limits to hunters. Fortunately, everybody else was gone.

By *everybody,* he meant Darcy. How much time had passed since she and her aunt had walked out? Logan had been so focused on not paying attention that he couldn't be sure. Ten minutes? Twenty?

He got in the van and was headed away from the event center when a third gunshot boomed.

That sound definitely came from in front of him, too close to the road. As a rule, hunters knew better than to fire willy-nilly, even when they thought the woods were empty. But people with the best intentions could be careless.

And this might not be experienced hunters. It could be kids messing around with their parents' firearms. Somebody could get hurt.

Darcy could get hurt.

Logan hit the gas, driving as fast as he dared on the winding road. His van, outfitted to haul food for events, had cost a few months' income. If he wrecked it, it could ruin his family's finances.

He forced himself to slow down. Darcy and her aunt were fine, probably back on the highway and headed to Portland by now.

And maybe, just a little bit, he was hoping to catch up with them. Maybe, just a little bit, he regretted not talking to her.

Just a little bit. *Right.*

Idiot.

At the fourth gunshot, all thoughts of romance fled. Not that he'd been thinking about romance. Not that he'd admit to anyway.

He was going to find that moron and...

What was that?

Something shiny caught his eye. He hit the brakes and twisted to get a better look.

Was that a car—in the woods?

He backed up.

Sure enough, a blue sedan was wedged up against a thick oak tree.

Logan pulled over, jumped out, and jogged to the wrecked car, slipping a jacket on over his T-shirt.

The backseat passenger window was broken, the glass intact but spiderwebbed with cracks.

But the opposite corner of the vehicle had hit the tree—the back fender. The car had been moving in reverse?

Why?

And how had the opposite window broken?

More to the point, where was the driver?

"Hello?" His voice carried in the quiet. "Everybody okay?"

No answer.

Weird.

This was less than a mile from the event center. Surely, the driver would know it was a shorter walk back to the building than down to the highway a couple miles below. So why hadn't Logan passed anyone walking up?

"Hello!" he called again.

He peeked into the driver's window. A little yellow-and-white brochure rested on the console. He opened the door and snatched the contract, fearing what it would say before he found the name.

Darcy Partington.

He dropped the contract and looked around again. Where was she? Where was her aunt?

He peered into the dark forest all around. What was going on?

He cupped his hands around his mouth and shouted, "Darcy!"

Nothing.

His heart raced. Why would they leave the vehicle, unless...?

The gunshots.

Had they panicked?

Darcy had always been level-headed, not one given to panic, though how would she react if she thought she was being shot at? No telling.

He searched for clues like some sort of detective. The window hadn't spontaneously broken itself. There was a small round hole in the web of cracks. His heart dropped into his stomach when he realized what it was.

A bullet hole.

The front tire was flat. Though he didn't bend to confirm, he assumed that it, too, had been shot out.

Somebody had fired at them. At Darcy. *His* Darcy. On purpose.

Why?

He circled to the passenger side. The rear quarter panel was dented. She'd been moving at a good clip—backward.

He could imagine the terror she must've felt.

This was no accident.

Random? Or targeted? Either way, Darcy and her aunt were lucky to be alive.

Were they alive?

Terror heated his skin. He itched to start searching, but where?

There was no blood, no sign that either Darcy or her aunt had been injured. They weren't with the car. Had they run—or been taken?

The passenger door was open. They must've climbed out on the opposite side from the shooter, based on the bullet hole. So probably not taken.

He peered among the oaks and pines and maples. The woods were thick, bushes and brush covering the ground. He was no tracker, but broken twigs and overturned leaves marked where the women had gone.

He didn't shout this time, not that it mattered. The shooter had to know he was there. Maybe Logan had already been targeted. Maybe the next shot would be aimed at him.

But Darcy was out there, on the run and in danger.

Logan had left his phone in the van. Even if he hadn't, it would be useless. There was no service on the mountain. And he wasn't leaving the women to fend for themselves.

He followed the trail silently. Praying for help. Praying he'd find her and her aunt.

Before a killer did.

CHAPTER FOUR

The faraway echo of Logan's call had long since faded. He must have seen the car. Would he leave before making sure they were all right? The old Logan would search until he found them.

Of course, the old Logan wouldn't have avoided talking to her.

Darcy had found MJ at the bottom of the hill, looking haggard but alive. They'd run, crashing through thorns and briars that ripped at their clothing and dug into their skin. They'd skirted trees and climbed rocks for fifty yards, maybe a hundred, with no idea where to go, where to hide.

And then Darcy had spotted a fallen tree, rotting on the ground. The thick trunk, propped up by its wide root system, had fallen over a small depression on the forest floor, creating a hidey-hole.

They'd all but dived into it. Now, they crouched side by side, backs to the hill behind them, gaze fixed between the broken branches and dead leaves, watching.

Listening.

As slowly as possible, Darcy pulled her cell phone from her

pocket. If she could reach the police. She dialed 911, praying the call would connect to *some* cell tower.

Apparently, no cell tower serviced this mountain. She put the phone back into her pocket.

For a few moments, they heard nothing but the natural sounds of the forest. Skittering squirrels and chattering birds. The rustle of leaves overhead. The buzz of black flies and mosquitos feasting on their flesh. As tight as their hiding spot was, they dared not brush the insects away for fear of making a noise or shimmying leaves.

Something snapped. A twig. Someone was coming. Logan? Or the shooter?

It wasn't as if they'd been careful or quiet when they bolted through the woods. They must've left a trail. They might as well have dropped breadcrumbs.

Her feet ached from her stupid shoes. MJ's low heels were a little more practical—but only by degrees.

It wasn't anywhere near dusk, but the overcast day provided scant light, and what did get through the clouds had to penetrate the forest canopy. Maybe the darkness would hide them.

But the footsteps came nearer.

MJ gripped Darcy's arm. Whatever happened, they were in this together.

Leaves rustled. The figure was creeping, getting closer.

A pair of legs clad in black denim moved into the view between the fallen tree and the ground. Only inches separated Darcy from the man.

She covered her mouth with her hand, afraid she'd gasp and give them away.

He stopped and turned toward them, close enough that, were she to reach out, she could touch his kneecaps.

And then a new sound came—the snap of a branch?

The man bolted deeper into the forest, his retreat much louder than his approach had been.

One was gone—to where?

Another was coming.

But who was who? Had that been Logan, close enough to touch, trying to avoid getting shot? Or was Logan the one coming now?

She had no idea and dared not peek.

Minutes passed, and then the quiet swish-swish of leaves and bracken.

"Darcy?"

The word was a whisper, quiet as the breeze.

MJ squeezed her arm and shook her head.

But Darcy recognized that whisper.

She pulled from her aunt's grip, jostling the branches overhead.

Suddenly, they were pushed aside, and a man peered down at them.

He had Logan's eyes, his beautiful eyes, the ones she'd tried to avoid all afternoon. They were filled with relief, and for one glorious moment, she thought, *Logan is here, and everything will be fine.*

Nothing bad could happen when she and Logan were together.

If they were together, then the world was set aright. The muddle was clear. The chaos was ordered. Life made sense again.

He reached down, and she took his hand and climbed out of the hole and around the branches. She stepped into Logan's arms. Inhaling his scent, both familiar and longed for, the scent of home.

He wrapped his arms around her and held her against his

chest. He spoke into her ear, his breath fluttering her hair. "Thank God. Thank God I found you."

They stayed like that, just like that, for a long, perfect moment.

And then he stepped away. Cold air and realization shocked her as Logan's gaze flicked downward, behind her. "You okay?"

"I think so." Darcy stepped out of the way, and Logan helped MJ from the hollow beneath the tree. When she was on her feet, he stared into the forest where, Darcy assumed, the gunman had run. There was no movement. No sign of the man who'd disappeared like vapor.

Even so, she felt...watched.

"What happened?"

She explained, quickly, how they'd been shot at and followed, and how the man had been there only minutes before.

"Why didn't you hit the gas and try to get out of here? Why back up?"

"He was in the road ahead of us. I was trying to get back." *To you,* but she didn't say so.

The gunman was out there. Biding his time. Seeing everything.

"Let's go." Logan nodded for them to go back toward the road.

MJ took one step but stumbled on her second.

Darcy grabbed her and kept her from falling.

Behind them, Logan asked, "What's wrong?"

"I twisted my ankle." MJ's whisper was frantic and terrified. "I don't think I can walk."

Darcy's heart stuttered and raced. MJ had tripped a couple of times on their run, but she hadn't realized her aunt had been injured.

Logan stepped in front of the older woman and crouched. "Hop on. Hurry."

MJ did, with Darcy's help, and Logan hitched MJ higher, his arms supporting her thighs, her hands gripping his shoulders.

Logan looked from MJ's feet dangling in front of him to Darcy's shoes. "Can you wear hers?"

Darcy's heels were definitely not practical. Unfortunately, MJ's feet were two sizes smaller than Darcy's. She shook her head, and he sent her Ferragamos a quick glare before turning away. "Stay low. Follow me." He started through the woods, moving more quietly than she could manage, despite carrying a grown woman piggyback.

Darcy followed, careful not to fall off her too-high heels and praying they'd make it to the retreat center before the shooter decided to finish what he'd started.

Because as much as she wanted to believe he was long gone, she couldn't convince herself. Not when she could feel the heat of his gaze boring into her back.

CHAPTER FIVE

Logan needed to focus. He needed to not think about what could have happened—and what still could.

Why would anybody want to kill Darcy or her aunt? It made no sense.

"Where are we going?" Darcy's whisper came from behind him.

He shook his head, trying to tell her without words to keep quiet. The woods wouldn't muffle her voice. Or her heavy footsteps, but nothing could be done about that. It was hard enough to walk along the forest floor in sneakers. He couldn't imagine trying to do it in her ridiculous shoes.

Were they being tracked? Was the gunman a would-be murderer, waiting for an opportunity to finish what he'd started?

Why had he run when Logan appeared? He was armed, and Logan wasn't. Why not just shoot him? If he was willing to kill women, what was one more body?

But maybe it wasn't about murder. Maybe he was trying to kidnap MJ or Darcy. Or send a message or...something. Even so, he'd come with a weapon and was obviously prepared to use it.

They needed to get back to the road and his van. Once

they did, Logan would put the women in the back and floor it to the highway. If the guy took a shot, he'd only be able to hit Logan.

Which... Yeah, he didn't want to get shot. His family needed him alive and healthy and working.

But at least Darcy would be safe.

For a minute. But if Logan was dead, the van would crash. The shooter would come and...

"Are we going to the retreat center?"

"The van," he hissed.

"Don't you think—"

"We need to put distance between you two and that guy. The van is the only way to do that."

"But at the retreat center, we can call for help, right? There're phones."

"If we get to the van, we can get out of here and get you two somewhere safe. The retreat center—"

A gunshot cut him off.

He ducked, dropping MJ behind him and yanking Darcy down.

The gunshot had sounded from up ahead, so he shifted the three of them behind trees, ensuring the trunks separated the women from the shooter.

Another gunshot. And then a third and a fourth.

Were the bullets aimed at them?

He didn't think so, but at what, then?

The answer felt obvious. The shooter was rendering the van, the only escape, useless.

Even if Logan's guess was wrong, the gunman was in front of them.

They'd be fools to keep going that way.

"We need to get back to the building," Darcy whispered. "We can call for help."

If driving out wasn't an option, that seemed the next best choice.

But that was the obvious second choice. If they climbed back up the low mountain to the building, they might be walking straight into a trap. If he thought they had any chance of beating the guy there...

The gunman had the ease of moving along the road while Logan was trudging through the woods carrying one woman while another teetered on stilettos.

No way they could beat the guy there.

He thought of the stocked kitchen, the comfortable chairs, the warmth. He thought of the phone that could summon help.

Then he released those thoughts like a helium balloon, letting them float away. Because going that way could get them killed.

Plan B...or was it C? They could hike down to the highway, but it would take hours to get there. And what if the gunman wasn't working alone? What if he had somebody watching for them?

Even if they reached the highway without being spotted, there was nothing for miles and miles in either direction. They'd have to stay in the woods, out of sight, until a car came along. And then hope its driver wasn't their shooter or an accomplice.

Plan D, Lord? Guidance?

Logan knew where he was. He knew where the road, the highway, and the retreat center were.

The shooter knew all those things too. The obvious destinations weren't going to work.

But Dad's hunting cabin might.

He closed his eyes and imagined the layout of the land. He'd hiked all over it as a kid. Miles and Linny had often joined Logan and Dad on day trips. Logan had been a couple years older than Linny, who'd followed him like a devoted fan. At first he found it annoying, but they forged a friendship, playing in the small pond while Dad and Miles sat in canvas camp chairs on the shore. Logan and Linney climbed rocks and even found a cave.

Of the four of them, only Miles and Logan remained.

If Miles were here, he'd tell Logan that God always made a way. He always had a plan.

Lead me, Father.

He'd never approached the cabin from this side, but he could find it. They'd walk toward the stream and then head upward, which would lead them to the pond. And to the cabin.

He faced Darcy.

And was rendered speechless at the sight of her, looking at him with those gorgeous eyes he'd fallen in love with.

They were beautiful. Bright green and filled with terror. And hope, in him.

She was disheveled, leaves in her hair, dirt on her face, and looking more like the little girl who'd become his best friend so many years before than the woman she'd grown into. The beautiful, beautiful...

He tamped down the errant, useless thoughts. "He'll expect us to go to the retreat center. Come on." He turned away from the road, away from the highway, away from the building.

"Where're we going?" MJ asked.

"Dad's hunting cabin."

"Oh." Darcy sounded...what? Surprised? Wistful, as if she remembered it like he did?

Obviously wishful thinking, considering her next words were "How far?"

He doubted she'd want to hear the answer. He didn't want to think about the miles between here and safety or the fact that he'd have to cover those miles with a grown woman on his back.

Darcy would have to cover the miles in high heels.

He'd never been a fan of reality TV because, really, who had time to watch a bunch of overgrown children play cruel games with each other?

Somehow, they'd landed in a bizarre *Survivor*-like episode. Except this was no game. This could be life-and-death. And it involved the woman he loved.

CHAPTER SIX

To Darcy, Maine meant splashing in the shivery surf. It meant volleyball on the beach and crabbing among the rocks. It meant late sunsets, grownups sipping wine while kids played tag until it was too dark to see.

Her Maine meant charming shops painted every color of the rainbow. Where the town grump refused to deviate from the ugly brown his grandfather had chosen *back when there weren't so many a you from away, muckin' up the place. Ayuh.*

Maine was souvenir T-shirts that cost twenty bucks apiece in June, two for twelve in August.

Lobster rolls dripping with buttah and mayonnaise. It was seafood chowdah and oysta crackahs.

Maine was not this squishy green world of dead leaves and live bugs trying to eat Darcy alive. She didn't even like to stray off the manicured trails in Central Park. She definitely didn't like the woods, all wild and shimmying with furry rodents and creepy-crawlies.

She only had one good memory of being in the Maine woods, and it involved the place they were going now. And the man leading the way.

The summer before they started college, Logan had taken her to his favorite fishing spot and then to his father's hunting cabin. She could still see the rough wooden walls and smell the musky scent of moisture and age. It'd been a cold evening in August—much like tonight—and he'd started a fire in the tiny woodstove. He'd brought sandwiches from Webb's Harborside, his family's restaurant. A turkey-and-provolone for her and a BLT for him—plus a couple of bags of chips. He'd laid a blanket on the floor in front of the stove, and they'd had a picnic.

And kissed. And talked about the future, and kissed some more.

There'd been a moment when she'd thought they might go beyond kissing. She was considering ignoring the vow she'd made to stay pure, believing with everything in her that Logan was hers, and she was his, and what difference would it make if they sealed that now?

But Logan, always the gentleman, had stopped long before the point of no return, uttering apologies and promising that someday, they'd do it right. *After the wedding.*

As if their getting married were a foregone conclusion. It had seemed so, back then. She'd have put money on it.

In a million years, she'd never have thought he'd leave her.

The hike was too quiet, the fears too close, and the man in front of her far too real. But she didn't feel the gaze of the gunman anymore, or hear any strange noises beyond the typical creaking and rustling of the forest.

The shooter was probably at the retreat center, waiting for them to show themselves. Because only a fool would trudge through woods toward...nothing.

The old hunting cabin was far enough off the beaten path that probably nobody knew it was there.

So this wasn't a terrible idea.

Except her feet were killing her.

Logan must've guessed that because, once they were a good distance from the cars they'd left behind, he stopped, allowing MJ to slide to the ground as he spoke to Darcy. "Give me your shoes."

"What? Why?"

His eyebrows hiked, and he held out his hands. They were killing her, and maybe he had a solution. She handed them over, standing on rough ground and thanking God for bare feet.

Logan snapped off a heel.

She gasped. Mom had bought her those shoes on a recent shopping excursion. They'd cost roughly ten times what Darcy would ever pay for a pair of shoes, even if she could afford it, but Mom had insisted.

And maybe Darcy had chosen to wear them this weekend because she hoped she'd see Logan, and the shoes were gorgeous.

Stupid choice all around.

They'd be worthless after this anyway, so she didn't react when he snapped off the other heel and handed the shoes back.

A lot of words came to mind, but she only said, "Thank you," and then dropped to her knees. "MJ, let me look at your ankle."

Her aunt settled on a rock, and Darcy eased her nylon sock off, earning a hiss. She studied the swollen ankle. It was straight, not sitting at an odd angle. A good sign. She probed the skin from the lower calf to the foot.

Though MJ didn't protest, she did stiffen in obvious pain.

"Any numbness?"

"No."

"Pins and needles?"

"No. It doesn't hurt unless I put weight on it."

"Good." She slid the nylon back on and looked up. "I think it's just a sprain."

"Thanks, sweetheart."

Logan was gazing at Darcy, head cocked to the side, a slight smile on his lips. "You get a medical license I don't know about?"

"One of my authors wrote a book about treating minor injuries and illnesses." She stood and brushed wet pine needles off her pants. "I put together a series of posts with some of her tips. Knowing the difference between a sprain and a break was one of them."

"A survivalist book?"

"Not exactly. It was for moms. You know, when should I take my kid to the doctor or the ER, and when should I just plop an ice pack on it and let him watch cartoons."

"Ah." Logan chuckled. "This is an ice-pack-cartoon moment?"

"I'd watch cartoons right now," MJ said. "Though no thanks on the ice pack. My feet are cold enough."

"What would you do if it was broken?" Logan asked.

Darcy shrugged. "According to the meme... Call 911."

"Lucky for us, then." He grinned, then helped MJ to her feet before turning and crouching. "Hop on, hop-along."

They continued the hike. The shoes were better without the height. She no longer felt as if she were traversing a bed of red-hot nails. Now, the nails were practically room temperature.

An improvement.

Two hours into their walk, she wondered if they'd ever get where they were going. And if Logan had any idea where they were. Because everything looked the same to her.

Brown tree trunks interspersed with an occasional white birch. Green leaves. Rusty pine needles littering the ground. Spiny, spindly branches scraping at her arms and legs.

Three hours into the walk, the late summer sun dimmed.

Yet Logan tromped on.

He'd warned them that the woods wouldn't muffle their voices much. Aside from that one stop, they'd barely uttered a word since they'd set out.

MJ still rode on his back, her head resting on his shoulder as if she might be sleeping.

Darcy would give anything to trade places, but her aunt's ankle was swollen to twice its normal size, so fat that Logan had taken off her shoe and shoved it in his back pocket. Better treatment than Darcy's heels had gotten. He'd hidden them beneath a pile of leaves. No sense leaving a trail.

She had blisters, and pain stabbed with every step. Though the shoes were easier to maneuver without the heels, they felt oddly off-balance, angled wrong. With the damp ground, she was at risk of slipping and falling with every step.

She desperately wanted to stop and never move again.

She'd keep going, even if the hike killed her.

By four hours into the walk, she sort of wished it would.

She was berating herself for the errant, ungrateful thought when her foot caught on a root. She stumbled, gasped, and went down.

She landed hard. The rough ground bit into her palms and knees, but being off her feet brought so much relief that she nearly cried. She didn't move, didn't even try to get back up.

MJ slid down beside her and sat, stretching out her injured ankle. "You all right?"

No. Not even close.

"I tripped," Darcy said.

"Ah. Thought you were doing acrobatics."

Darcy couldn't summon a smile.

Logan crouched in front of her.

She didn't realize how dark it'd gotten until she tried and failed to make out his features.

"Are you hurt?"

Tears stung her eyes. What was she doing here?

She should be in Manhattan, feet on her coffee table, sipping an ice-cold root beer. She should be binge-watching some terrible TV show. She'd be alone, of course. She spent a lot of time alone. But at least she'd be warm and dry.

Instead, she was sitting on wet ground in the dark in the middle of nowhere, crying like a fool. Did she think somebody would scoop her up, nestle her close, and carry her?

There wasn't a soul in the world who cared for her like that. Hadn't been in a long, long time.

Logan bent lower to be at her eye level, allowing her to pick up the shadows of his face. He looked concerned. "What can I do?"

"I'm sorry." Her voice was high and squeaky and all wrong. She cleared her throat. "Sorry." If she kept saying it, maybe he'd stop looking at her like that.

MJ wrapped her arm around Darcy's back. "Don't apologize, sweetheart. If I hadn't sprained my ankle, your Logan would be carrying you."

"Not *my* Logan." She hated the snappish tone, but she didn't need more reason for tears. And she didn't need him looking at her as if he cared. She knew better. A decade of silence had taught her better. "I just need a break."

Logan sat and stretched out his legs beside her. "Next time, just tell me you need to stop." The concern was gone from his voice. In fact, he sounded annoyed. "I can't haul both of you."

"I'm fine. I just need—"

"A break," he supplied. "We heard."

She bent her legs and tugged off one shoe. The relief was instant and acute and nearly had her crying again. She tugged off the second, rested them both in her lap, and leaned back on her hands.

The cool air hadn't bothered her when they were walking,

but now a chill had her fighting a shiver. Everything was damp. The ground. The trees. The fabric of her pants. Her legs.

"You don't happen to have a sandwich in your pocket, do you?" MJ's question was lighthearted, but the need behind it was no laughing matter.

Darcy's stomach had been growling for hours.

"Got a bunch, in the van."

"Run back and get us a couple, would you?"

Logan chuckled. "Let's call for takeout. I could go for a nice, thick steak."

"Make that two," MJ said. "And a baked potato with all the fixings. I'll even spring for extra bacon."

"Fries." Logan's voice took on a dreamy quality. "Crispy and salty, with mayonnaise for dipping."

"Mayonnaise?" MJ sounded scandalized. "What kind of commie puts mayo on their fries?"

Darcy and Logan had had this conversation a thousand times. Like any red-blooded American, she preferred ketchup.

"Don't knock it," he said. "The French use mayo, and they know a thing or two about *french* fries."

"If that were my *only* choice"—by her tone, MJ sounded horrified by the prospect—"I guess I could force down a couple."

"With a nice summer ale," Logan added.

"Iced tea, please, lightly sweetened with a slice of lemon."

Their silly chattering gave Darcy a moment to pull herself together after her little breakdown. They were all alive, all safe. Logan was with them and had a plan.

She was thankful. Truly, she was. Now that she wasn't in pain, she could focus on that gratitude.

"You're both wrong," she said.

"Hmm?" Logan said.

"What would you order?" MJ asked.

"Shrimp fettuccine Alfredo, crisp Caesar salad, warm garlic

bread and…" She knew the perfect pairing and could even name the winery and year. Manhattan had more than its share of wine snobs. How many arguments—Napa versus Sonoma versus Whatever-Pretentious-Region, France—had she endured over the years? When wine was offered, she sipped and made the appropriate noises because that was what one did when dining with the elite. But, if she were to choose an adult beverage without fear of raised eyebrows, she'd choose a wheat beer with an orange slice.

What she really wanted at that moment? "A tall glass of ice water."

Logan sighed. "We'll reach a stream eventually."

"How much farther, do you think?" She hated to ask the question, hated playing the part of the whiny kid in the backseat. But it would help to know they were closing in on the cabin.

"I'd say we're about halfway."

Halfway!

She dropped her head to hide fresh tears. She'd never make it. She wasn't even sure she could get her shoes back on her swollen, blistered feet.

"I miss the old Darcy," Logan said, "with the flip-flops and sweatshirt and shorts."

"We're not seventeen anymore. I have a job."

"Stilettos are part of the uniform for"—he waved his hand toward her—"whatever it is you do."

"They're not stilettos. Just…shoes. I'm a publicist."

"That requires three-inch heels?"

"It requires that I look professional." She emphasized that last word. "Some of us don't get to wear sneakers to work."

"Some of us can be professional in sneakers." He bent his one knee and yanked off a shoe.

"What are you doing?"

"My socks are wet and disgusting, but they're cushioned." He pulled one off and held it out to her. "It won't protect against sharp things, but maybe—"

"I can't take your socks."

"Too gross for your professional publicist sensibilities?"

She didn't miss the dare humming in his words.

"You need them," she said.

"I have shoes."

"You'll get blisters."

He sighed. The sock still dangled between them. Though she couldn't make out his face, she could feel the glare. She glared right back.

She didn't know why. She should be thankful, but old hurts didn't fade easily.

MJ said, "For heaven's sake, sweetheart, take the socks. You know you want to."

Yeah, well... She snatched the one and slid it over her foot, wincing as the fabric rubbed the torn blister on her heel.

But oh, once it was on, it felt so good.

He handed her the second and then put his sneakers back on. "Can we go on now?"

"MJ had a good idea." Darcy didn't know if she could keep going, and maybe, if he wasn't saddled with them, he could move faster. "She suggested you run back to the van."

"I was kidding!" her aunt said.

"I'll get right on that," Logan deadpanned. "Roast beef or ham and Swiss? We ran out of turkey."

"I'm just saying, what if MJ and I find a place to hide and you take my phone and—"

"Your phone? You have your phone?"

"Yeah." She fished it from her pocket and lit the screen.

He snatched it and flipped it over, pressing it against his pants. "Don't light it up. We don't want to be seen."

"If the guy's close enough to see that, he already knows where we are."

Her remark was followed by a long pause and then, "Even so, save the battery."

"Or," she ventured again, "you could take it and go somewhere where there's service. MJ and I will stay—"

"I'm not leaving you alone."

"If we hide—"

"No." His tone was serious, bordering on angry. "I'm not leaving you to fend for yourselves."

"It's not your job to save the world, Logan."

The instant the words were out of her mouth, she wanted them back.

They were the words of the argument that had ruined everything.

His response reverberated now. *Not everybody is made of money. They need me.*

And then Logan had walked out of her life. She'd thought their separation would be temporary. One semester until Logan's dad got back on his feet or they made other arrangements for the restaurant. But one semester had turned into two, which had turned into forever. Just like that.

Darcy could feel her aunt's gaze boring into the side of her head but didn't dare look. To Darcy, MJ was her beloved aunt—and her most successful client. But every once in a while, MJ looked at her in that *psychologist* way she had.

I know what you're doing.

I know why you're doing it.

I see right through you.

As if Darcy were a puzzle to solve, and not a particularly complex one.

But MJ didn't say a word.

Neither did Logan. Darcy didn't dare guess what he was thinking.

She hadn't apologized back then because she'd been certain she was right.

Young, foolish, naive—but certain. Why apologize for speaking the truth?

She'd matured since then. "I'm sorry. I didn't mean—"

"It's fine." Logan pushed to his feet and brushed his hands off on his pants before reaching toward MJ. "You ready?"

MJ looked at Darcy for a long moment, then took his offered hand and stood.

He crouched, and she hopped on his back.

He looked down at Darcy. "Stay here if you want. Don't feel obligated by my savior complex."

"I didn't mean... I'm so thankful you saved us."

Her words bounced off his back as he walked away.

By the time she got to her feet, he and MJ were disappearing into the darkness.

CHAPTER SEVEN

It's not your job to save the world.

Nice of Darcy to twist the knife still lodged in his heart. Even after ten years, she didn't understand.

He trudged forward in the pitch-black night, moving slowly until Darcy caught up. They weren't going to break any speed records. They spent half their time circling puckerbrush and climbing over fallen logs. His legs were aching from carrying MJ, his feet scraping raw inside his shoes.

But his thoughts were on that terrible time a decade before.

If something had happened to Darcy's father, she and her mother would barely miss a beat. The two of them had always been close, more like sisters or friends than mother and daughter. Meanwhile, Darcy's dad was off on his private jet, making money and deals and enemies, leaving his wife and daughter to fend for themselves. They didn't count on him for anything but income. It was one of the reasons Darcy had loved hanging around Logan's family when they were kids. She'd marveled at Logan's dad, who'd been involved in every aspect of his kids' lives.

His mom and dad had been partners and best friends.

When Logan was a kid, he and his siblings had their own table at the restaurant. Mom was always there, overseeing their schoolwork and helping Dad when he needed it.

Dad would sit with them whenever he had a spare minute, helping Jewel with her math or Laine with her grammar or Ryder with his handwriting.

When Logan was fourteen, Dad started training him in the family business, not because he wanted him to work there but because he wanted him to have an excellent work ethic and understand how to operate a business. Dad taught Logan everything from how to make batter and fry fish to how to evaluate financial decisions and balance the books. When Jewel was old enough, Dad had invited her to help as well.

Mom and Dad had laughed and labored together, side by side, working to achieve the same goals.

Once upon a time, Logan had dreamed he could have a marriage like theirs. He'd imagined the business he would run and the family he'd help educate and train.

He'd even picked out the wife.

Dad's stroke had changed everything.

Logan had been in his second year at NYU. Jewel had been thirteen, capable of bussing and waiting at the restaurant but little else. At ten and seven, Laine and Ryder couldn't help at all.

Dad's stroke left him unable to even feed himself, much less run the family business. Mom had needed to care for him.

If the great Master Partington had needed a caretaker, Darcy's mom would have hired a nurse. Probably a whole team of nurses. No problem for someone worth hundreds of millions of dollars.

Unlike the Partingtons, the Webbs didn't have a literal fortune in the bank.

So Logan had left school to help. Did that mean he had a savior complex? Or proper priorities?

"She didn't mean it, you know." MJ's voice was low in his ear, too low for Darcy to hear.

"It's fine."

"She's just scared and hurt. But she understands."

"Mmm-hmm." Sure she did.

Except every conversation after he'd left school to help his family had been stilted. They'd never gone back to the friendship they'd enjoyed before, much less the romance.

And his one attempt to fix that had ruined everything.

"I should try walking," MJ said. "My ankle's better."

"It's not."

"If we could find a walking stick—"

"You're light as a feather."

Her laugh sounded forced.

"You two okay?" Darcy asked.

"Your... Logan is being stubborn."

"Business as usual then," Darcy said, going for lighthearted as if her accusation wasn't hovering between them.

He backed up to move a branch out of her way. This was no easy task, considering he was using his arms to hold up MJ.

Darcy stepped past it. "I just wanted to say—"

"It's fine." He moved in front of her to continue leading the way.

How long had they walked since their last stop? He couldn't check his watch without dropping MJ and didn't want to ask Darcy because... Well, just because.

"Will your family miss you if you don't make it home tonight?" Darcy asked.

"I live alone."

"Oh."

Apparently, she'd pictured him still living with his mommy.

"You went home to help take care of your siblings," she said, "so I figured—"

"I run the business. Mom manages the kids." Maybe his curt tone would discourage her from asking questions.

But this was Darcy.

"Jewel looks great," she said. "I can't believe how old she is. She said she finished college?"

"Yup."

"What'd she major in?"

"We should be quiet in case your friend is out here."

"If he can hear us, he's already too close."

Probably. They were keeping their voices low, and they'd heard nothing that indicated there was anyone nearby except woodland creatures and bugs.

MJ supplied the answer. "Jewel majored in hospitality management."

Logan asked, "How do you—?"

"We had a nice chat at lunch. She's a sweet girl. Said she wants to help run the family business."

"Really?" Darcy said. "That'd be great."

"Why?" He sounded...churlish and grouchy, like the lonely old man he was destined to become.

"Because..." Darcy, on the other hand, suddenly seemed unsure of herself. "Don't you want to go back to school and finish your degree?"

"I'm happy where I am." Yeah, that was it. He sounded *so happy*.

"Oh."

A few minutes of blessed silence followed her single syllable, and then, "Where do you live?"

He managed to keep the heavy sigh between himself and MJ, who giggled, apparently enjoying the show.

"In the apartment over the restaurant."

"You're kidding." Did Darcy have to sound so horrified? "That place was a dump."

When they were children, they'd crept into the musky old rooms more than once, playing games among the broken-down and moth-eaten furniture left by the building's previous owners.

Dad had talked about redoing it for years, but running the business and taking care of his family had taken all his time.

"I remodeled it." Three little words that couldn't begin to cover the hours and hours of work. It'd taken weeks just to haul away the previous owner's junk. Logan had knocked down walls and replaced the sixties-era kitchen appliances. He'd changed the old cabinets and chosen granite countertops. He'd scraped popcorn ceilings and refinished hardwood floors. With the help of friends—and Google—he'd turned the old dingy space into a beautiful, modern apartment.

"I'd love to see it," Darcy said.

And just like that, he could picture her there. In his mind's eye, she wore gym shorts and an NYU sweatshirt, standing on the new third-floor balcony above the restaurant. She was staring out at the Atlantic. Wind in her hair. Smile on her face. A twinkle in her eyes like she was plotting some silly adventure.

He tried to rekindle the anger he'd felt a few minutes earlier. But dang it, she was being so nice. It was annoying.

"So nobody will notice if you don't make it home tonight," Darcy clarified.

"I won't be missed until tomorrow when Jewel shows up at the restaurant. You?" He infused the question with a casual tone, as if it didn't matter if there was a boyfriend waiting up for her. As if it wouldn't kill him.

"Mom'll worry when I don't call tonight," Darcy said, "but she'll assume I forgot. She won't panic. And I'd already planned to work from home tomorrow."

MJ said, "I won't be missed until a midafternoon client."

Good to know they were all so important.

"You think somebody will come looking for us in the morning when you aren't at work?" Darcy sounded optimistic, as if rescue were just a few hours away.

"I think so, eventually. They'll find my van and your car, and then..."

"The shooter will be long gone." The confidence in the older woman's voice surprised him. "We just have to find a place to hide. There'll be searchers out looking for us."

"Yup."

"But?" Darcy must've heard something in his response because she sounded wary.

"But nothing," he said. "Once we get to the cabin, we should be fine for a day or two."

"Or two?" MJ echoed. "It'll only be a few hours, don't you think?"

"There are acres and acres of uninhabited forest out here, most of it inaccessible. It'll take them time to find us. Once we get to the cabin, we'll need to stay, just in case that guy is still looking for us."

"Won't they check the cabin?" Darcy asked.

"We don't advertise its existence, considering this isn't our land. My grandpa built it before all this was turned into a state park. Nobody ever made him tear it down, but technically, it probably isn't supposed to be there. I don't think Mom even remembers where it is. She and my sisters hate hiking. I've brought Ryder up here a couple of times, but he wouldn't be able to find it. Miles would."

"Miles O'Neil?" MJ asked. "I thought that was him today."

"Yeah. He was Dad's best friend. He runs the retreat center, so I'm sure the authorities will call him when they realize this is where we went missing. He can direct the police to us. It's a matter of how long it'll take before it occurs to him that we might've gone there."

His words were followed by a whole lot of silence.

"Sorry to disappoint," he said. "But it won't help to worry. God got us away from that shooter. He got us this far. He'll make a way."

"Yes, well..." MJ didn't sound convinced by that. She squeezed his shoulders. "I trust you'll get us out of here."

Trust him. Not God.

Hadn't MJ been a believer? He'd thought so.

And Darcy said nothing. Back...before, she'd been a woman of faith. Had she lost that? Had living in New York and rubbing shoulders with faithless friends and coworkers changed her?

<h1 style="text-align:center">CHAPTER EIGHT</h1>

D arcy had always admired Logan's ability to talk about God—and *to* God, for that matter—as if He were right there, leaning in, eager to hear what His child had to say.

As if there were no question of His existence.

She believed in God. And for a while, after the church camp in high school when she'd asked Him into her heart, she'd read her Bible and prayed every morning.

A lot of years and disappointments had come and gone since then.

These days, God felt more like a distant relative she'd met once or twice, an eccentric uncle whose stories she'd heard around the campfire, but someone she could pass by on the sidewalk without a second glance.

God was a stranger to her. And maybe she was a stranger to Him too. Would He recognize her if they were on the street together? Would He stop to talk to her? Or walk on past?

Was the real God like the one Logan believed in, an attentive Father eager to be with His children?

She doubted it. The Divine's thoughts toward her were probably filled with disappointment—if He thought of Darcy at all. And why not? He'd blessed her with so many advantages, and what had she done with them?

Not enough. She'd never been enough for her own father. Surely, God's standards were even higher.

She hadn't been to church in years. She hadn't prayed, and truth be told, she wasn't sure she could put her hands on her Bible on a bet. Was it on the shelves in the tiny living area? Maybe buried under all the books on her nightstand?

Did it matter?

Maybe God cared about some of His people, but obviously she wasn't one of them. Case in point: She was trudging through the woods wearing nothing but socks, her feet frozen and numb, the rest of her body racked with chills. Hungry, thirsty. Trying to avoid a madman with a gun.

If there were a God who loved her, wouldn't He help?

"So," Logan said—and she didn't miss the false cheer in his voice—"any idea who's trying to kill you?"

"You don't think it's random?" MJ asked. "Some crazy person?"

Darcy hadn't given much thought to who the gunman was, being so focused on trying to get somewhere safe and warm. But now that he asked, she forced herself to consider the question. MJ's answer didn't sit right.

"It's possible." But Logan sounded less than convinced.

"I'd hate to think someone wants me dead," MJ said, "but I do get some rather interesting mail. No actual death threats though." She tossed the words over her shoulder. "You'd have told me, right?"

Darcy was glad her aunt couldn't study her face in the darkness.

One of Darcy's tasks was to sort through the letters and emails that came in for MJ, most of which had been sent by adoring fans or people who wanted something—interviews and advice being the most requested. But there were crazy people in the world, and MJ's books sometimes rubbed them the wrong way.

She recalled some of the more explicit and threatening letters, which she'd passed on to the publisher, who forwarded them to law enforcement. She assumed the threats were filed in case something terrible happened.

Like a shooter in the woods, for instance.

Before she could explain all of that, Logan stopped abruptly. "Wait."

"What is it?" MJ whispered.

"You hear that?"

Now that he mentioned it, Darcy did hear something. A distant gurgling.

"Finally." He moved forward again, and they walked in silence for five or six minutes while the sound got louder and louder.

Logan moved around a huge bush, and MJ held it aside so Darcy could pass.

She did and reached the edge of a stream. It was tiny, easily hopped across, the clear water tinkling over rocks and reflecting moonlight.

She hadn't realized the clouds had dissipated, but in the narrow clearing, the sky and the half-moon spilled enough light to cast a shadow.

MJ slid off Logan's back, Darcy supporting her until she was steady on the uneven ground.

None of them spoke as they knelt beside the water and sipped from cupped hands.

Darcy moaned with pleasure when the first few drops hit her scorched throat. She hadn't realized the enormity of her thirst until that moment. Now, she drank and drank, wondering if she'd ever get enough.

Logan sat back on his feet. "We're going to stay near the stream up the hill, so no need to overdo."

Reluctantly, Darcy dried her wet hands on her slacks.

"Let's rest a few minutes."

His words alone were a balm. She sat back on the grassy ground, and Logan settled beside her. With the moonlight overhead, the soothing stream bubbling nearby, and Logan close enough to touch, she felt almost...safe.

MJ pushed to standing, and both Darcy and Logan started to get up.

"I'm fine. The ankle's better already. I'm going to find a bathroom." Darcy didn't miss the humor in her voice. "I'm sure there's one around here somewhere."

"Let me help." The last thing Darcy wanted to do was stand on her aching feet, but MJ was injured.

"Young lady." MJ infused her voice with false parental irritation. "I have been doing this by myself since I was two."

"But just to—"

"I'm fine." To prove her point, she hobbled into the woods, using tree trunks as supports. Soon enough, her bright red suit disappeared in the darkness.

Logan watched, too, and then looked at the stream meandering past. "Mind if I ask you a personal question?"

"I guess not."

"Are you seeing anyone? Or...has there been someone?"

Heat skimmed over Darcy's skin, though she couldn't say if it was fueled by fear or hope. That Logan asked, that he cared—

"Usually, violent acts are committed by people we know," he added. "Loved ones or... Well, not *loved,* I guess. But you know what I mean. That is, if cop shows are to be believed."

Oh. He wasn't asking because he cared. He was trying to figure out who'd shot at them.

Disappointment sloshed in her water-filled stomach. She

worked to keep her tone even when she answered. "As far as I know, nobody wants me dead. If someone did, he'd kill me in Manhattan, not follow me to Maine."

"Not if he wants to throw off the police. Who knew you and MJ would be here this weekend?"

"It was on her website. All her speaking gigs are."

"Even though it was a private event?"

Darcy shrugged. It hadn't been necessary to promote it, but it was important to show the world how valued and sought-after MJ was. As her aunt's publicist, Darcy put every interview and speaking gig on the website.

"Do you always attend with her?"

"Usually, if the events aren't too far from New York. She's not the only author assigned to me, but she is the biggest seller, and she likes me with her."

"Who knew *you'd* be here this weekend?"

"People I work with, of course. The editor, the publisher, the travel coordinator. Outside of work?" She paused to consider. "My mother. A few friends." And then she remembered the Instagram post she'd sent from LaGuardia. "I posted that I was traveling, but not to where."

"But if somebody were to look at your aunt's schedule, they'd be able to guess. So if somebody is after you—"

"Nobody's after me, Logan."

"No ex-boyfriends?" When Darcy didn't answer, he bumped her shoulder. "It's been a decade. I'm not going to be mad."

"I didn't think that." Not mad, anyway. Jealous, maybe. She would be, but she figured his feelings hadn't lingered like hers had. "I've only had one boyfriend since you. We dated for about a year."

She didn't miss the way his lips pulled at the corners, the cringe. As if she'd wounded him.

"I thought it was casual," she continued. "It was for me. A plus-one for weddings and Christmas parties. Someone to see a movie with, you know? But I guess he was more serious."

"You broke up with him?"

"Six months ago." She should leave it at that. But something compelled her to speak the rest. "After he proposed."

If she'd expected a reaction, she'd have been disappointed. Or maybe the way Logan froze, his face suddenly devoid of emotion, *was* the reaction.

He swallowed, his Adam's apple dipping and rising. And then, "Was he angry?"

"He was disappointed." When she'd turned Jonas down, he'd seemed angry. He'd loomed over her, eyes blazing with fury, but she'd assumed he'd acted that way to hide his hurt and embarrassment.

She'd been amazed at how quickly he'd gone from love to hate.

"And?" Logan's tone was gentle, as if he guessed she was hiding something.

She shouldn't say anything else, but the words were demanding to be spoken. Because Logan was here. With her.

And Jonas had seen right through her.

"He accused me of harboring feelings for you."

Logan shifted to face her. "You told him about me?"

"Not exactly. It's just..." What was she doing? Was she trying to make him jealous? She needed to stop, now. She wasn't a tween girl, and this wasn't some silly crush. This was Logan, her Logan. The best friend she'd ever had. If not for their failed romance, he'd probably still be her best friend.

Their romance had ruined that. Except, at the time, it'd felt like the natural next step. How could she not have fallen in love with him?

But all that was in the past now—the friendship, the romance. She needed to keep it there, where it belonged.

"The point is," she said, "he was angry. He said I used him as a placeholder. Which... Obviously not, but I never cared for him like he cared for me. So I can see why he thought that. If I'd known..." She sighed. "Anyway, I apologized, and he went away. I haven't seen him since."

"Six months is not that long. He could be..." Logan's voice trailed as MJ hobbled back to join them. He stood and helped her ease to the ground.

"You telling him about Jonas?"

Logan's eyes popped wide.

Darcy's heart fell.

"Not Jonas Barton." He directed the question at Darcy, the name spit like one might a particularly offensive curse word.

"He grew up," Darcy said. "He changed."

"He was obsessed with you."

"We were old friends, that's all. He wanted to continue our friendship and—"

"Despised me because we were together. He was—"

"A kid, Logan. Just a kid. An immature, spoiled teenager who didn't know how to handle a little crush." Back in college, Jonas had tried to horn his way in between Darcy and Logan. He'd made overtures—discreet at first—toward her. He'd tried to turn her against Logan. When that didn't work, he started a rumor about Logan and another woman.

"He's a psychopath." The growl in Logan's voice wasn't lost on Darcy—or MJ, whose eyes widened.

"It was stupid, childish stuff," Darcy said. "After you went back to Maine, I reiterated my lack of interest, and Jonas left me alone. I ran into him a couple of years ago at a wedding, and he apologized for everything."

"And you believed him."

"He was sincere, Logan. Jonas has nothing to do with this. He wouldn't hurt me."

"Forgive me if I don't take your word for it."

"Whatever." She stood and marched away, refusing to limp on aching feet. Not that she needed to find a private tree. Just a break from Logan, who'd reacted just like she'd known he would.

He was jealous.

A petty part of her was happy. A hopeful part of her wanted to believe it meant something.

And that made her the biggest fool in the world.

CHAPTER NINE

Logan was the biggest fool in the world.

While he'd been living like a...what had Jewel said? A cloistered monk? Darcy had been dating.

Jonas Barton, of all people.

Logan despised the man who'd tried so hard to destroy their relationship back in college. When the lies that he'd cheated on Darcy with another girl had amounted to nothing, Jonas changed tack. He told people Logan had sexually assaulted a younger student at a party. He'd gone so far as to offer the freshman money to tell campus police that Logan had forced himself on her.

And who would have doubted the young woman? As a rule, people believed such stories, even before the me-too movement. The freshman in question came from a wealthy family with long ties to NYU.

Unlike the full-scholarship kid from Maine.

Thank God she'd had a moral backbone or Logan might've not only been kicked out of college but ended up in jail.

He'd never told Darcy the extent of Jonas's lies because the freshman had asked him to keep quiet. She had been embarrassed about the whole thing and wanted the story to die away.

Logan had been beyond grateful for her honesty and had never told a soul. Eventually, Jonas's rumors had fizzled.

Logan should have told Darcy everything. Would she still have dated the man if she'd known what a snake he was?

"You all right?" MJ whispered.

"Fine."

She opened her mouth to argue, then tipped her head to the side.

He heard it then, an engine. Getting louder. And closer.

He jumped up and scooped MJ into his arms, eliciting a squeal of surprise.

"What if it's help?" The older woman's eyes were wide with fear. "Maybe we should—"

"It's not help." He huffed into the woods, heading in the same direction Darcy had gone.

Where is she?

He didn't see her and didn't dare call out. Probably, the gunman wouldn't be able to hear him over the roar of the engine, but he wasn't taking any chances.

Behind a thick bush, he set MJ down, slid off his charcoal jacket, and draped it over her. "Get under that and stay there." He was breathing hard from the run.

"Find Darcy!"

That was the plan, but the engine was closing in, fast.

Where is she?

Movement to his left, closer to the stream, caught his attention.

Darcy stood behind a tree, looking toward the noise.

Logan darted that way. "Down, down!" he hissed.

She turned toward him, eyes wide with surprise.

He swept her off her feet and dove, cushioning her fall with his arms. He rolled over her, shielding her with his body.

Face down, Darcy struggled to crawl out from beneath him.

"Be still. Please."

"Where's MJ?" She turned her head to glare at him. "I have to—"

"She's fine."

His knees and bare forearms were chilled on the damp ground, but Darcy's body beneath his was warm even as she continued to struggle. "Let me go."

He whispered in her ear. "If you give us away, you could get us all killed."

"But MJ—"

"She's hidden. She's deeper in the woods. He won't find her."

The words had her settling beneath him. "What if it's someone trying to rescue us?"

A valid question. Could it be?

But nobody would've discovered him missing yet. And the women weren't due back to New York until late. So he doubted the person on the dirt bike was there to rescue them.

The engine roared, then it cut off suddenly.

Logan could guess why.

He'd gotten too comfortable, believing they'd left the gunman behind. They'd lingered beside the stream, making no effort to hide their presence. The moonlight probably cast shadows over their footprints.

He dared not look but imagined what he'd see as he listened to the noises. The scrape of metal was probably a kickstand. A whoosh, probably a branch being pushed aside, then snapping back.

Footsteps would be silent on the damp ground. Meaning the person could be moving farther or coming closer.

Then the snap of a twig that sounded from just a few feet away.

Beneath him, Darcy seemed to shrink like a turtle into its shell.

If the stranger came close, he would see Logan's blond hair and light skin poking out of his T-shirt.

Help, Lord. Please.

Lying on his stomach, he felt completely vulnerable. Not that anything he did could protect Darcy from a bullet.

He heard the man breathing. So close. Surely, they'd be seen.

He waited for the boom of a gunshot. A shocking pain in his back. Would it travel through him and into Darcy? Would she be killed or only injured until his body was pushed away so the killer could finish her off?

He should've hidden away from the women, somewhere he could attack, maybe disarm the killer.

An error. *Not a fatal error, please.*

And then, as quickly as he'd come, the gunman moved away from them.

It was another few minutes before the engine roared to life and the man drove slowly away.

Darcy squirmed, and he realized he'd lowered onto her, his own attempt at becoming smaller.

He shifted to hold his weight with his arms to keep from crushing her. "Be still."

Because what if the gunman wasn't alone? What if somebody else watched, waiting for them to show themselves?

No, he didn't move and prayed MJ would be still.

As the sound of what had to have been a dirt bike faded, other sensations came to life.

He blamed the terror of the moment for his heightened senses. Darcy's back pressed against his chest, warm and familiar. Her hair tickled his cheek. Her floral scent overpowered the musky forest, muddling his mind when he needed to remain focused.

How many nights had he dreamed of her in his arms? How many mornings had he prayed the Lord would take away his love for her, only to dream of her again?

And here she was. He peered down at her long, straight neck, the curve of her chin, the pink of her cheeks. It was all he could do not to lower his head and press a kiss to that soft skin. He could almost taste the salt of her.

Memories of so many kisses flooded over him. The promises they'd made to each other. The love they'd professed. God help him, as much as he'd tried to redirect his affections, his love for her hadn't faded.

He wasn't an arrogant kid anymore. Life had weathered him, matured him, and humbled him. He'd changed, but his love for Darcy hadn't. If anything, it'd matured too.

He wanted her. Not in his arms or in his bed. He wanted her in his life, forever. Just like he always had.

"Do you think he's gone?" she whispered.

And just like that, he was back to himself. Back to the man who'd chosen duty over desire.

She was still the woman who hadn't understood.

He looked around for any sign that a killer remained. When he saw nothing but tree trunks and bracken, he rolled away. Staying low, he scanned the area. But they were alone.

She sat and looked at him, her face filled with fear. "How do you know that wasn't a rescuer?"

"They'd have called out."

"Oh. Right." She cast her gaze around as if the guy might be right there. "You think we're safe?"

"For now." He held out a hand and pulled her to her feet. "Sorry about... I didn't want him to see you."

She brushed dirt off her clothes, then looked around. "Where's MJ?"

Logan trudged back to where he'd left Darcy's aunt. "It's us," he whispered as he neared.

The older woman sat up and held out the jacket he'd given her. "We're safe?"

"Let me make sure. You two stay here." He slipped his jacket on as he headed back toward the stream just thirty yards away. The man had been too close.

"Did you get a look at him?" Darcy was on his heels.

"I didn't dare." He turned to face her. "I'd rather you stay with your aunt."

She reached out and slid her hand over his arm. "Thank you for"—she nodded toward the place they'd hidden—"protecting me."

"You're wel—"

"But next time, stay with MJ. I'll blend in more with my black than she will in that red suit. And she can't run with a sprained ankle."

A lot of responses came to mind. Logan wanted to tell her he'd gone to her because MJ had told him to—which was true.

That Darcy had been more vulnerable because she'd been closer to the stream—which was true.

That, dark clothing or not, her blond hair stood out in the darkness—which was true.

But none of those things had occurred to him as he'd bolted toward her and practically tackled her onto the forest floor. He hadn't thought about his own safety. He'd barely considered MJ's. All he'd thought at that moment was...

Save Darcy.

And he couldn't promise that he wouldn't do exactly the same thing if it happened again.

"Would you stay with her, please?" he asked.

Darcy stared up at him, studying him through narrowed eyes. And then she trudged back to her aunt.

Logan crept forward. The grasses were pressed down where they'd sat near the stream earlier. No wonder the gunman had noticed.

Tire marks confirmed what Logan had guessed—a dirt bike. It'd come from higher up the mountain, traveling alongside the stream.

He hopped the water to the far side and saw where the man had turned west. He must've assumed Logan and the women had gone that way.

So... how to throw him off?

Logan jogged downstream, careful to stay close enough to the trickling water that his sneakers left prints for a good fifty yards. Then, he jumped and did the same on the far side before he headed into the woods, where leaves would cover footprints.

Maybe that would help, because soon enough, the gunman would realize he'd lost their trail and return to where he'd last seen it.

Logan retraced his steps, hopped the stream, and moved into the woods, where he hurried back to where he'd left Darcy and MJ. "We need to move."

Darcy, who'd been staring toward where he'd gone earlier, whipped her head toward him. "Where did you...? What are you doing?"

"Trying to throw him off."

She stood and helped MJ to her feet.

Once Logan had the older woman on his back, he turned in the opposite direction from where he'd left the false trail. They'd stay parallel to the stream, but they wouldn't be able to get near it again until they reached the cabin.

Only as they hiked in silence did the full weight of what they'd learned press down on him.

Of all the places the gunman could've searched, he'd looked for them here. Dumb luck? Maybe.

With a dirt bike, the shooter would be able to cover far more ground than Logan and the women could. Yes, they'd be able to hear him coming. But if they weren't careful, they could leave a trail that would lead him right to them.

CHAPTER TEN

Nobody spoke for a long time.

Darcy didn't know what kept MJ and Logan quiet. In her case, she couldn't stop remembering the sound of that twig breaking just a few feet away. If not for Logan's body pressed against hers, she'd have panicked. He'd not only protected her but hemmed in her terror.

Now, as the wind blew through her, all the fear of that moment whispered in her ear.

She focused on the stream gurgling nearby, though Logan kept them a good distance from it. They were moving upward on a gentle slope, farther and farther from the road that ringed this low mountain. If Logan hadn't been here, the killer would have found them by now.

Maybe killed them and left their bodies for scavengers.

Would Logan keep them alive? Or would his body be with theirs after the gunman caught up with them?

She hadn't prayed in years, distancing herself from the God she knew couldn't possibly love her. Even so, she hoped He listened to the steady calls for help she silently sent upward. *For MJ's sake, and Logan's, please save us.*

Not for Darcy's, though. She knew better than to expect anything from Him.

"You okay back there?" Logan's voice was barely audible over the wind as he trudged in front of her, clearing the way.

"Fine. You?"

"Yup."

A few moments passed, and then MJ spoke. "You never said, Darcy. Have I received death threats?"

She'd always shielded her aunt from the hate-filled emails and letters she opened. "Just the usual."

Logan stopped and turned to face her, "The usual...what?"

"She gets threatening letters sometimes. Her books have sold almost a million copies. It's bound to happen."

"Nothing serious, right?" MJ asked.

Since her recent book had released, people had written claiming her philosophy—which was all about people seeking their own happiness before trying to seek that of others—had ruined marriages and broken up families. Some had taken MJ's ideas too far.

"Well?" Logan prompted.

"Not everybody understands—"

"Darcy." Logan's voice was insistent. "Has she gotten death threats?"

"Not death threats, of course." MJ's tone was unconcerned. "Some people don't like what I have to say, but nobody wants to kill me. Right?"

Darcy had to work to hold her aunt's eye contact. "You have your share of...detractors."

"What do you mean?" MJ's eyebrows hiked.

Logan's lowered, casting his eyes in shadows.

Darcy focused on him, unwilling to see how the truth would hurt MJ. "There've been some death threats, but it's not *that* unusual."

He took that information in. "Anything credible? Anyone you'd take seriously?"

She shrugged, trying to look nonchalant. "That's not for me to decide. I send them to the publisher."

"And then what?" Anger infused his words. "You just pretend they don't exist?"

"What should I do?" Darcy asked. "Hire full-time security?"

"Yes." The word was hissed as much as spoken.

"I didn't know." MJ sounded horrified. "Why didn't you tell me?"

"It's my job to deal with it. It's my job to protect you from that. If they'd thought there was anything to worry about—"

"Who is *they*?" Logan asked.

"The publisher sends them to law enforcement."

"Who probably don't even look at them." Logan huffed as he turned and continued their trek.

Darcy stayed on his heels, feeling as if this were her fault. As if she'd been the one to pen those letters and type those emails.

Maybe it *was* her fault. She shouldn't have been so cavalier about the death threats. But a lot of authors got them, the successful ones, anyway. And Darcy wasn't trained in the art of analyzing crazy people. How would she know which were credible and which weren't?

That'd be a great defense if MJ got shot.

"I'm sorry." She spoke to her aunt's back. "I should have told you. I trusted that if there was any real danger, Howard would do something about it."

"Who's Howard?" Logan asked.

"My publisher," MJ explained. She twisted to Darcy and added, "It's not your fault. I wrote the book."

"I should've talked to him. Lately, there've been letters that were more...concerning." She didn't want to elaborate on that.

MJ looked over her shoulder. "I'm sorry you have to deal with those, sweetheart. But you don't have to protect me. Besides, I'm sure they were all just empty threats."

Darcy was pretty sure she heard Logan scoff.

"You're right, of course." MJ responded to Logan as if he'd spoken his thoughts. "Someone is shooting at us. At me, I guess. If anything happens to either of you—"

"Or you," Darcy said. "You're a world-renowned psychologist, beloved by millions."

"Hated by a few."

Darcy ignored that. "People depend on you. Not just the people you help but... How many salaries do the sales of your books pay? How many other books are able to be published because of the income you generate for the publisher? And Logan. You've got a family to support. They count on you. If anything happens to either one of you, and I could've prevented it..."

A burden settled on her shoulders like a wet wool mantle. Too much responsibility. How would she live with it if her negligence got either one of them hurt or killed?

She'd followed procedure and trusted that Howard would intervene if MJ were in real danger. But had Howard even read the letters?

If Howard had forwarded them, had the cops or FBI or... whoever he sent them to bothered to peruse them? Or were the letters sitting in some inbox somewhere, untouched and unread?

How could Darcy not know the answer to that? What a poor excuse for a publicist—and niece—she'd turned out to be.

Just like she'd been a poor excuse for a daughter. And a poor excuse for a girlfriend.

Would she never get anything right?

CHAPTER ELEVEN

Between the death threats MJ had received and the fact that Darcy had recently rejected a marriage proposal from a psychopath, there were too many options for who might be trying to shoot them. Not that the *who* on the other end of the rifle mattered that much. Once they were safely off this mountain, law enforcement could figure that out.

Logan's job was to keep them all alive until then.

Even in the moonlight, the forest started to feel familiar. Sure enough, they reached the base of the rocky slope he used to climb as a kid. He'd climb it today if not for the woman riding piggyback. And the other one wearing nothing but wet socks on her feet.

He skirted the steep rocks and found a slightly easier way, though it still required climbing.

"You up for this?"

Darcy gazed up at the slope, determined. "Lead the way."

He searched for the easiest path, but there was nothing easy about navigating this in the dark. At least not much vegetation grew here, though he did nearly slip on a patch of moss.

"Careful there," he said before Darcy reached it. "Avoid that spot."

He watched to make sure she didn't fall, then continued. "You're going to have to hang onto me," he told MJ.

"You can put me down," MJ said. "I can manage it."

"Just hang on, please."

She squeezed her legs around his waist and gripped his shoulders tighter, and he grabbed a skinny tree trunk for balance.

He reached the top, huffing for breath. Apparently, his daily exercise hadn't prepared him to haul a hundred-something-pound woman up a mountain.

"I know that wasn't easy."

He'd answer her if he could catch his breath.

MJ slid off his back, and Logan turned to check Darcy's progress. When she got near enough, he reached down to help her.

She grabbed his offered hand, and he hauled her up. He pulled too hard, though, and when she was on solid ground, she stumbled forward, crashing into his chest.

"Whoa." He wrapped his arms around her to keep her from falling.

And a thousand memories hit him. He and Darcy, just like this. On the beach. In the waves. On MJ's balcony. In his living room.

A thousand perfect moments.

The images were a gut-punch, so shocking he was surprised he didn't lose his breath all over again.

"Sorry." She looked up at him with wide eyes. He saw fear there. Of him? Of all the feelings that must've shown on his face? Or did she feel them too?

"My fault." He let her go and stepped back, forcing his gaze away, onto anything else.

He shouldn't have done that. He shouldn't have allowed that. Because now all he could think about was how perfectly she fit in his arms. And how he could get her there again.

"Wow." MJ's voice was filled with wonder.

He turned toward her, thankful more than he could express that the older woman was there to distract him.

Then he shifted his gaze to the pond in the distance.

The older woman hobbled from trunk to trunk toward it. "It's beautiful."

Small and secluded, it was bordered by tall pines and oaks and birches all around. Moonlight shimmered on the placid waters and made it look magical.

Darcy caught up with her aunt and helped her to the shore.

He'd brought Darcy here once, years before, on a day not too different from this one, though it'd been a sunny afternoon, not a cool night.

Did she even remember?

"There was a little pond like this not far from where I grew up." MJ turned to Darcy. "Your dad and I learned to swim in it."

"Dad, in a pond?"

Logan didn't miss the disbelief in her tone and tended to agree. Mr. Partington was more the Jacuzzi or steam room type.

"He loved it. There was an island." MJ laughed, the sound lighthearted and girlish. "We called it an island, but really, it was just a tiny bit of land that disappeared when the water rose. We used to race to see who could swim to it fastest. When I won, he'd claim he let me. Which he probably did."

"Dad? *My* dad?"

MJ shot her a surprised look. "He was a kid once, you know." She faced the water again, her tone turning wistful. "He was fun and tenderhearted. And hilarious. He was always goofing around."

By the shock on Darcy's face, she couldn't imagine. "What happened to him?"

MJ's smile was sad. "Dana. His death changed everything."

If Logan hadn't been watching Darcy so closely, he'd have missed what flashed in her eyes. Of course she still grieved the older brother she'd lost. But there was more to that look than sadness. He saw raw agony.

He shouldn't want to find out what had put that look on her face. And he shouldn't want to fix it.

But he did.

Carrying MJ again, Logan traversed the familiar—if overgrown —trail from the pond to the cabin, covering ground faster than they had all day.

Finally, he spied the hedge of brush. "We're here."

"Uh…" MJ sounded skeptical, not seeing what was obvious to him.

Logan continued toward the bushes that seemed to have grown haphazardly around the small building, remembering the summer he and Dad had planted them. They were prickly, chosen to keep people out.

He found the opening, which was barely wide enough for him to pass through after years of neglect. "Tuck in." MJ did, and he pushed past sharp branches, holding them aside so Darcy could follow into the clearing around the stone cabin.

"Oh!" MJ said.

Darcy stepped up beside him. "It looks just the same."

So she did remember. He tapped MJ's leg. "Hop off so I can get the door open."

She slid to the ground, and he approached the corner of the

cottage and ran his fingers between the rocks, praying he wouldn't find some creature's home.

Instead, he found the cold metal key and unlocked the door. "Wait here." Inside, he let his eyes adjust, then scanned the space, looking for the flashlight he kept on a table near the door. He found it and flicked the button.

He turned and held the flashlight out to Darcy. "You remember where the outhouse is?" At her nod, he said, "You can use it while I get the rest of the lamps lit."

The disgust on Darcy's face mirrored that of her aunt.

"Or just find a secluded bush on this side of the hedge. Come in when you're finished." Not that he liked leaving them alone, but as long as they stayed close to the cabin, they should be safe.

Darcy and MJ hobbled toward the old outhouse, and he returned inside.

He located a couple of battery-operated lamps to further brighten the space. It wasn't impressive, just two little rooms with pine floors and stone walls separating inside from out. An old sofa sat beside a wood-burning stove that had a black chimney rising to the vaulted ceiling. There was a heater in the corner. The propane tank was empty, though. He'd meant to take it to be filled the last time he was here, but he'd forgotten.

On the opposite side of the room, a metal closet rested beside cabinets and a countertop where they prepared food. On the other wall, a door led to the bedroom.

When Darcy helped her aunt inside, he stepped forward and took the older woman's hand. "Come on in. It's not much."

"Are you kidding?" The older woman hobbled toward the sofa and collapsed. "I've never seen anything so beautiful in my whole life."

"That's what we in the biz call hyperbole." Darcy sat next to her aunt. She yanked off the socks that had to be soaking wet and smiled at him. "Thank you for getting us here. This is perfect."

"Far from." He closed and locked the door, then carried one of the electric lanterns into the bedroom.

Two twin beds had about a foot between them. Near the door, a cedar chest was closed and latched. Inside, Logan found blankets and pillows that seemed no worse for the neglect. He quickly made up both beds, then dug back into the chest, where he found fat, fluffy socks, along with sweatshirts and sweatpants. Dad's old clothes, and a few that Logan had left when he was still in high school, kept here just in case.

He pushed the door closed, toed off the sneakers that had worn blisters into his heels, stripped off his damp jeans and T-shirt, and traded them for clean clothes. Dad's things were a little snug but warm and dry.

He draped his damp jeans and T-shirt across the cedar chest and left the rest of the old clothes on one of the beds for Darcy and MJ.

He grabbed the extra blankets and carried them to the other room. "There're dry clothes if you want to change."

Darcy pushed to her bare feet. "Definitely."

"You two get comfortable while I look for something to eat."

"You have food?" The hope in MJ's voice had him wincing. He should've kept his mouth shut.

"Maybe." After the women closed the door to the bedroom, he turned to the kitchen—called that because of the counter and cabinets, even though there were no appliances or sink or running water.

There was hand sanitizer, which he squirted onto his hands before opening the metal closet doors.

Bottles of water. He set four on the floor near the couch

then sucked down another, thankful for the cool moisture on his dry throat.

He'd hauled supplies up that spring, planning to use the cabin as a getaway when the weather warmed. He'd craved—still craved—time away from work and family. Not that he didn't love his mom and sisters and brother, but they always needed him for something—repairs around the house, rides here or there, help with homework.

Was it terrible to want a break sometimes?

He'd even planned to bring Ryder and teach him to fish like Dad had taught him.

But summer hadn't turned out like he'd hoped. The restaurant had been busier than ever, and the few days Logan had been able to take off, he hadn't had the energy to fill a backpack, much less hike into the forest with his little brother.

So the supplies were still here, just waiting. Lots of cans—soup, beans, vegetables. Also canned ravioli and O-shaped spaghetti.

He dug into the cabinets beneath the linoleum countertop, looking for the propane-powered stovetop he vaguely remembered Dad buying but never using. He and Dad always cooked over a campfire.

They couldn't do that tonight, nor could they fire up the woodstove. The scent would lead the shooter right to them.

No sign of the stovetop. Hungry as he was, cold ravioli didn't sound too bad.

He raised the flashlight and checked the top shelf.

And imagined the angel choir singing as he pulled the bags down.

Gorp.

That was what Dad had always called this stuff.

Normal people call it trail mix, Dad. Nobody calls it gorp.

Dad's response: *You calling me a nobody?*

Logan smiled as nostalgia rolled over him. He could hear humor in his father's voice as he chided Logan for picking out the chocolate pieces. He felt Dad's huge hand ruffling his messy little-boy hair, telling him it was okay. He could have all the chocolate he wanted.

The door between the rooms opened, and Logan shook off the wave of grief. Darcy looked tiny in his old gray sweatpants and sweatshirt that had to be three sizes too big for her. There was nothing attractive about the outfit. So why did the word *adorable* float through his mind?

"Pay dirt." He pulled a bag down, then checked the expiration date. "Dang. It expired."

"What is it?" Darcy asked, coming up behind him.

He lifted the bag of nuts, chocolate, and dried fruit.

She took the bag from him and checked the date. "It's fine."

He shifted to face her. "You sound so confident."

"An author I work with wrote a book about how much food we waste in the US. That"—she nodded to the tiny print on the package—"is one of the reasons. Food manufacturers are required to give expiration dates, but there are no guidelines. They're often chosen at random. And manufacturers err on the side of caution."

"Wise. Keeps people from eating bad food."

"And it encourages them to throw away perfectly good food —and buy more."

"Let me guess." He held out his hand, and she gave him back the package. "Did you create memes about that?"

"Wrote a blog post."

He smiled. "There's hand sanitizer there"—he nodded to the bottle—"and water by the sofa."

MJ exited the bedroom in cozy, oversize clothes that used to belong to Dad. A bright yellow Bruins sweatshirt and a pair of gray pajama pants.

He slit open the top of the trail mix.

When they'd cleaned up as well as they could and draped one of the blankets over themselves on the couch, he said, "I'm sure the dishes need to be rinsed so... open your hands."

MJ did, and he poured some of the crunchy, sweet, and salty treat in there.

"You, Logan Webb, are my hero," the older woman said.

"Thank my dad. He was always lecturing me about keeping the place stocked in case of emergency."

Darcy held out her hands, and he gave her some of the treasure, then plopped on the floor, resting his back against the wall.

"You can sit with us," Darcy said, scooting closer to her aunt.

"This is fine. I'm not getting up again." Now that he was off his feet, he had no intention of moving.

He pulled the second blanket over his legs, then poured some of the food into his hand and ate.

He wasn't sure he'd ever tasted anything so good.

Darcy and MJ must've agreed because for a few minutes, the only sounds in the cabin were the quiet crunching of nuts and the occasional pouring of more.

By the time they'd emptied the bag, he felt satisfied. "There's bags of this stuff, if you're still hungry."

"Not me," MJ said. "That hit the spot."

"The clothes are okay?"

"Warm and cozy," MJ said.

"What's the plan?" Darcy asked.

"We should be safe here. This place is well hidden."

Darcy pulled her cell phone from her pocket. "Is there service?"

He managed to stifle a chuckle. "I know this feels like the Ritz, but we're far from civilization."

"We're higher up, so maybe..."

He didn't say anything, just let her discover the sad truth on her own.

A moment later, she shoved the phone back into her pocket. "It was worth a try."

"Of course it was, dear." MJ patted Darcy's thigh, then yawned and rested her head against the back of the couch.

"We should probably get some sleep." He stood and held out his hand. "Lemme help you."

The older woman hobbled beside him into the bedroom and to the closest bed. "Thank you."

"Sure. Let me know if you need anything."

"Logan?" MJ's voice was low.

He turned at the door. "Yeah?"

"I mean... Thank you for all of this. I don't want to think about what would have happened if not for you."

He didn't want to think about it either. Or how he was going to get them off this mountain. "I'm just glad I was there."

Her smile seemed almost sad. "I think..." She shook her head, and the expression morphed. Still a smile, but he didn't believe it for a second. "My ankle will be better tomorrow. We'll hike out, right?"

He wasn't sure. Would the gunman give up, believing they'd escaped the mountain? Or should they assume he was still out there somewhere?

Were they still being hunted?

"We'll decide in the morning." After he prayed about it tonight. If ever he needed God's input...

"You really think we're safe here?" Despite the twisted ankle, MJ had seemed strong on the trek. She'd been compassionate and gracious. She'd been helpful and lighthearted.

Now, though, she sounded afraid, almost like a child seeking reassurance from a grown-up. Had her confidence been an act for the sake of her niece?

An even scarier thought—the person she sought for reassurance was him. As if he were in charge of their protection.

"I think we're safe." He prayed it was true.

Back in the other room, Logan pulled the metal closet away from the wall. Dad had loved hunting, but he'd never wanted to keep his weapons at the house. Nor had he wanted them easily found if someone discovered the cabin. So, he'd purchased a gun safe and fashioned a false exterior. To all the world, the metal closet looked like that and nothing else.

Only someone who pulled it away from the wall and looked at the back would see that there was a narrow safe hidden there.

He unlocked it and swung it open.

"What's that?" Darcy's voice came from the opposite side of the door.

"Come around." He stepped away, and she did, eyes popping wide at the weapons. He asked, "You remember how to shoot?"

"Of course, not that I ever do."

He'd taken her to target practice a couple of times when they were kids. She'd been a decent shot.

"Get what you want. And something for your aunt. There's ammo on the top."

She chose Dad's old handgun and one of the rifles, leaving the Ruger, the larger, least sleek of the pistols. Maybe she remembered it was his favorite. She set the weapons and a couple boxes of ammo on the counter, and he closed and locked the safe, then pushed the metal closet back against the wall.

He loaded both guns, leaving them on the counter. When he returned to the living area, Darcy was on the couch again, her face lit by the glowing of her phone.

Would she ever admit defeat?

"You should get some sleep."

She nodded, but her focus didn't shift.

"You're not going to—"

"One sec."

He settled beside her, yawning and longing to stretch out on the too-short sofa and close his eyes.

And pull Darcy down beside him and cuddle. And kiss.

And tell her everything.

That thought propelled him back to his feet. He crossed his arms. "There's no service, Darce."

"I thought maybe..." She looked up, seemed momentarily confused to find him so far away. "Come look."

He sat beside her again, keeping as much space between them as possible.

She scooted close. "I found the death threats. I thought maybe—"

"You have them? With you?"

"In my email, yeah. Some were handwritten, but I scanned them before I forwarded them along. That's policy."

"Okay."

She tapped one of the emails. "This woman sent a few."

The image displayed big, loopy script. He took the phone and enlarged it, reading the letter that detailed how MJ's book had caused her husband to divorce her and how she was going to make MJ pay for her evil.

Three pages filled with threats about how the woman would kill MJ. Except none of the threats mentioned a gun. Or the forest. In fact, they were all very city-centric. She threatened to push her in front of a moving train and knife her in the street.

Random and scattered, obviously the ravings of a very angry person who had no real plan.

"Swipe to the left. They're all in there."

Logan did.

The next was an email from a man complaining that his fiancée had called off the wedding to pursue her own happiness because of MJ's book. The man vowed to make sure MJ never had a day of happiness again.

"What are her books about?" Logan had never read one. Even when he had time to read, self-help psychobabble wasn't exactly his genre.

Darcy sighed. "They're about knowing and accepting and loving yourself."

"And pursuing happiness?" he guessed, based on the letter.

"That's the problem." She whispered when she continued. "Her latest book goes too far. When I read it... I mean, I know her. I know what she meant. But I can see how people took it the wrong way."

"Like...how?" He couldn't imagine how a self-help book could cause this much trouble.

"She says we're all responsible for our own happiness."

"Sure. It's not one person's job to fulfill another person or make them happy." He could tell by the look on Darcy's face that he'd missed the point. "What?"

Darcy's gaze darted to the doorway. "There's a section in the book where she argues that people have to make themselves happy, even if it requires sacrifices. That we owe it to the world to pursue our happiness. She likens it to when you're on a plane and they tell you to secure your own oxygen mask before helping a child."

He considered that—and the ramifications.

"She didn't mean it the way people took it." Darcy defended her aunt as she gestured to the phone. "She wasn't telling people to leave their children and husbands. She wasn't telling people to neglect their responsibilities. But she also didn't exactly tell people *not* to do those things. I think she thought it was understood, but some didn't understand. Which… She isn't to blame if some guy walks out on his wife, claiming he has to go find his happiness. But—"

"It sounds like she was encouraging just that." They were both whispering now. He wondered what MJ would think if she overheard.

"It wasn't what she meant. You heard her talk today, right?"

It took a minute for him to figure out what Darcy was asking, probably because the event back at the retreat center felt so far away—in distance and time—from where they sat now. "I wasn't paying attention."

"Oh. Well, she said the same thing she's said over and over—in interviews, at events like today's—that true happiness should be found *in* our obligations. That when we rise to challenges, we grow. And that running away from our commitments isn't the answer."

"But not everybody sees those."

"She's written blog posts and been in magazines and been on talk shows." He didn't miss Darcy's defensive tone.

Apparently, lots of people had gotten the wrong idea from MJ's latest book and made terrible decisions because of it.

"Her editor should've caught it before it was published," Darcy said. "He was in the middle of some ugly life stuff, and he just…blew it."

"She blames him?"

"MJ? Not at all. She thinks the whole thing is ridiculous."

"When people are leaving their families?"

"She can't be blamed for that. People are using her book as an excuse to do what they'd already planned to do—or wanted to do anyway. At least that's what she thinks. But Howard blamed Xavier—and fired him."

"He *fired* him?" Howard was the publisher. Xavier must be the editor.

"And I heard from Howard's assistant that he led Xavier to believe MJ insisted he be let go."

"Why would he do that? Why lie about her?"

Darcy sighed, the sound exhausted. Logan got the impression the entire situation exhausted her. "Xavier is Howard's nephew, and he's trying to keep the peace in his family."

"By throwing your aunt under the bus?" If Xavier blamed MJ for his losing his job, then... "Could he be responsible? Could he be the one out there?"

"Oh." She blinked and looked toward the curtain-draped window. "I don't...know. They were close, MJ and Xavier. He'd been her editor since her first book twelve years ago. She was devastated when he lost his job. But, except the day he left, he hasn't spoken to her. And that day... He was upset. He said some things I'm sure he didn't mean."

"Like?"

"He told her she'd be sorry, that she'd regret getting him fired. She was too shocked to even defend herself. I know she's sent him a couple of emails since then, but he hasn't responded. He's still mad, I guess, but I can't imagine that he'd try to harm her."

"Is he a hunter?"

She shrugged. "I work with authors and the marketing team. I don't have much contact with the editors."

Logan took that information in. Maybe this Xavier was angry enough to kill.

If not him, then one of the people who'd emailed her?

He returned his attention to Darcy's phone and read page after page of threats.

Some were serious. Some vague. All designed to frighten, though some hit the target and others were almost laughable.

There was authentic rage. There was a lot of whining and casting blame.

But were any of these people actually killers?

Why would someone who truly intended to kill MJ warn her in advance?

Darcy watched the screen as he scrolled. After a few minutes, she said, "I thought maybe one would hint at hunting or...you know, Maine or something."

"I don't see anything like that." He kept going until he reached the image of an email. It was short and to the point.

It's all your fault, and you're going to die.

No signature, but that wasn't unusual.

What *was* unusual was that there was no salutation.

He scrolled back. Every letter before that had addressed MJ in some manner.

Dear Ms. Partington.

RIP MJ.

MJ Partington, you're about to die.

But this one didn't mention the author at all. The writer could be speaking to anyone.

"How do you know this one is directed at your aunt?"

Darcy tapped the addressee. "That's her email address."

Okay. But...

"Did you ever tell Jonas about the death threats?"

She shifted away. "Why?"

Logan didn't explain, just waited for the answer he knew she'd give.

After a minute, she said, "He's a lawyer. We talked about the threats because I was curious about whether or not it's illegal to send death threats and if so, what can be done?"

"Is it? Illegal?"

"Not in New York. There's a law about menacing, but the person has to be in a position to do the harm they're threatening."

"Jonas told you that." At her nod, he said, "So he knew."

"I don't know why that matters." Her tone told Logan she understood *exactly* why it mattered.

"Let's assume for a minute that he wrote that note."

"Why would he?"

Aside from the obvious fact that she'd rejected him, and he was a psychopath... "I don't know, Darce. Why would he?"

She seemed prepared to argue, then gazed at the note again.

He added, "How hurt was he? What could be all your fault?"

"He was embarrassed," she said. "He put together a whole... thing and invited all our friends and people he worked with, including his boss and his boss's boss."

Meaning Jonas had been pretty sure of himself. Either that or he'd known she might turn him down and thought she wouldn't dare in front of an audience.

Logan could imagine Jonas in either scenario.

"When I said no, he was furious." She took a deep breath. "It was ugly. If I'd had any reservations about my answer before, his reaction proved I was right to reject his proposal. I'd never seen him like that."

Logan had seen Jonas like that. He'd been apoplectic when he discovered his plot to have Logan tossed out of school—and arrested—had failed.

Logan had waited for him to throw a punch, but Jonas was more of an attack-from-behind kind of guy.

Darcy explained how Jonas, after her rejection, had called her names, accused her of all sorts of terrible things—like using him, cheating on him, and still being in love with Logan. "His friends tried to calm him down, but he shook them off. His boss finally stepped in. Jonas pulled himself together and apologized, but the damage was done. He made a spectacle of himself in front of coworkers and a couple of partners at his firm. A few weeks later, I heard he was passed over for a promotion he'd been assured was his."

So, not only had Darcy turned Jonas down, but because of his childish reaction, he'd missed out on an opportunity.

And blamed Darcy.

And maybe hated her enough to kill her.

CHAPTER TWELVE

If Jonas was as bad as Logan said he was, then Darcy was a fool.

Why had she believed he'd changed?

The answer was too pathetic to put into words.

He'd been interested, and she'd been lonely.

She only saw her father at the holidays—and even then, they barely spoke. Though she talked to Mom every day, they rarely saw each other in person. Darcy had friends at work, but nobody she was close to. And Logan, her best friend in the world, had left her.

Not that he hadn't had good reason. Was that supposed to make it easier?

When she'd seen Jonas a couple years ago, he'd apologized for the shenanigans he'd pulled when they were in college.

He'd seemed sincere.

She'd known Jonas as long as she could remember. Their parents were close, and she and Jonas had gone through school together. Maybe they hadn't always been great friends, but they'd been acquaintances with lots of people in common. When they were at NYU, she'd been surprised by his attempts to separate her and Logan because she'd never known he was interested in her, but also because his behavior had seemed out of character.

The Jonas she'd seen later had been charming and humble. He'd been like the kid she'd grown up with, making it easy to pass off his strange behavior in college as an aberration.

Had she really been so wrong about him?

She pushed to her feet and paced. "If it really is Jonas out there... If he's after me, then all of this is my fault."

"No," Logan said. "*If* it's him—and we don't know anything for sure—then this is *his* fault."

She waved those unhelpful words away. "You know what I mean. I brought this on us."

"You did nothing wrong. And it could be your aunt's editor. It could be any of these people who threatened her." Logan tapped her phone, still in his hand. "It could be anyone."

"But if it's my fault and something happens to either one of you..." She imagined bullets flying. Her aunt collapsing. Blood spreading over Logan's chest.

The images stopped her in the middle of the room. She squeezed her eyes closed and pressed the heels of her hands against them.

A moment later, Logan's arm slid around her back. "On the off chance the shooter finds us, it won't be your fault."

"If I thought it would protect you two, I'd just..." She opened her eyes and stared at the door between this comfortable space and the scary world outside.

"What?" Logan's arm dropped, and he stepped out of reach. "You'd what?"

"To keep you two—"

"Don't do that."

"I'm just saying." She paced away from him. She had enough of her own anger directed at herself. She didn't need to add his. "You and MJ are important. You're necessary. Your lives matter. If my leaving could protect—"

"Your life matters."

Of course he'd say that, but he didn't understand. "It's not the same, Logan. Nobody depends on me."

"What are you talking about?" He took a step toward her, moving into her space. Not only close enough to touch but close enough to feel. His heat. His breath. His frustration.

She backed away but bumped into the counter.

He retreated, a little.

"I'm just saying—"

"That your life isn't important?"

"You know what I mean."

"I don't. I can't even fathom."

She dropped her gaze to the floor. Was he really going to make her say it?

Apparently, because he didn't back down or back off.

"I'm just a publicist." She met his eyes, though it wasn't easy.

He tilted his head to one side. A moment passed before he spoke. "You're not *just* anything, Darcy. You're not defined by your profession."

"That's not what I'm saying."

"What are you saying, then?"

Cheeks burning, she scooted past him and returned to the sofa, where she pulled a blanket over herself. She didn't know how to explain what she meant. What she knew was that, if she were to die, the world would keep on spinning, and aside from Mom and MJ and a couple of casual friends, nobody would grieve her. She would leave no mark. Her life had made no difference.

Logan seemed rooted to his spot. "Please, explain what you mean."

She swallowed a lump of shame. "It doesn't matter. Let's just…" She flicked her hand his way, desperate for him to move on.

Instead, he approached and crouched in front of her. "Sweetheart."

"I don't need you to make me feel better. I don't need you to pretend."

"I don't have to *pretend* anything. What did you say? That you're *just* a publicist? As if that's all you are? It's not. You're also a daughter and a niece and a friend. Even if you were none of those things, though… Even if your family didn't exist or were too stupid to care about you…"

Logan had no idea how true his words were.

"Even then," he said, "you would be invaluable because you are a child of God. He created you for a purpose. He has a plan for you, and He loves you. Have you forgotten that?"

"He's forgotten me."

"He hasn't." Logan's words were confident, as if there were no question. "How can you doubt that?"

"My life isn't like yours, Logan. You've always been loved and treasured. Your father adored you. I'm sure your mother still does, and your siblings worship you."

One corner of his lips turned up, a fleeting smile. "Obviously, you didn't spend much time with Jewel today."

Darcy'd had a short conversation with Logan's sister, during which Jewel spent most of the time talking him up. "She admires you."

"She thinks I'm too protective. She's probably hoping you'll distract me."

Darcy grinned, but her amusement didn't last. She laid her head on the back of the couch. "It's fine."

Logan settled beside her and took her hand. "Please tell me what you're thinking."

Tears dripped from her eyes as she stared at the ceiling. She was so tired. That was the only explanation for the grief that felt so close.

"You remember I told you about Dana?"

"Your brother?" Logan said. "You were seven when he died?"

"He was nine, my hero and my best friend."

Logan shifted to fully face her on the couch. "A brain tumor."

She was surprised he remembered the details. "It happened so fast. He started complaining of headaches, and Mom took him to the doctor, who recommended...I don't remember. An MRI or a CT scan? Anyway, they diagnosed the tumor and..." She remembered her parents' shock. Her mother's grief and her father's fury at the doctor's prognosis. He'd railed at the man's incompetence, then made calls. He'd been determined to find someone who'd get the tumor out. But there was nothing to be done.

"He was diagnosed in September," she said, "and he was gone by Thanksgiving."

"Wow." Logan lifted her hand to his chest and held it there.

Her breath caught. It was something Logan would have done back when they were together. It felt so normal, so natural.

"That must've been awful," he said.

She swallowed emotions she didn't want to seep out. "Mom and Dad were so...sad. We were together, but separate, and it seemed like none of us knew how to reach the others. At the time, I couldn't have put into words what it felt like. But a few years later, Mom and I met Dad on a business trip in Hawaii. We were at Waikoloa on the Big Island, and my mom pointed out Maui across the water. The island was so close, but there was an ocean separating it from us. That's what it felt like when

Dana died—like we could see each other, but there was no bridge, no way to connect."

Logan nodded slowly. "I can't say that what our family went through was the same, but we all grieved differently when Dad died. Everybody had a unique relationship with him, so when we lost him, we each lost something different."

"I bet your family figured out how to grieve together."

He shrugged. "We tried to support each other."

Darcy remembered Mr. Webb's funeral. She and Mom had flown in and attended with MJ. The three of them had sat near the back. At that point, Darcy had still hoped she and Logan might mend the rift in their relationship. They'd been talking a lot, even if they hadn't seen each other in the months since he'd left school and returned to Maine.

The day of the funeral, she'd watched Logan's family at the church and then later at the gravesite. At only twenty years old, Logan had been the rock of the family, physically supporting his mother when she looked like she might collapse. Looking after his siblings. He'd stepped in like the caregiver he was.

He'd been amazing, but so had the rest of the family. Jewel had looked out for Laine, and Laine had looked out for Ryder, and all of them had stayed close to their mom. They might've been grieving separately, but they'd been one unit. A family, in it together.

Not like Darcy and her parents. Her mom and dad barely spoke after Dana's diagnosis, and even then, only about logistics and planning. There'd been no conversations about feelings. There'd been no shared grief or even shared memories.

The night after Dana's funeral, Darcy had lain awake, missing her brother and trying to understand what it meant. At only seven years old, she hadn't been able to comprehend the finality of it. All she knew was that Dana was gone, and everybody was sad because he wasn't coming back.

As much as she missed Dana, she also missed her mother and father, who'd barely acknowledged her all day. She'd been desperate for Mommy's hug and for Daddy to tell her that everything was going to be all right. She'd wanted to ask if Dana was in heaven like the minister said, and what heaven was like, and what Dana was doing. Could he see her? Could he hear her? Would he be sad without her?

She'd wanted Mommy and Daddy to tell her that she'd see her brother again one day, that he wasn't really gone forever.

When she heard her parents talking—for real, for the first time in a long time—she crept down the stairs, thinking she'd crawl onto Mommy's lap and just be with them.

But she wasn't supposed to get out of bed after they tucked her in, and she didn't want to get in trouble. So she settled on the stairs, out of sight but able to listen.

Now, she explained to Logan, "Just hearing them talking made me feel better. Knowing they were together made me feel...safe."

He squeezed her hand, still pressed against the warm fabric of his sweatshirt, his attention fully on her. It had been so long since anybody had looked at her like that, like she was the most important person in the world.

"But Daddy was upset," she said. "I think he was crying, which he hadn't done at the funeral or even when Dana died. And he said..." Her voice rose and squeaked. "He said that Dana had been gifted and brilliant and...and I was just average."

"What?" Logan's shock was replaced by tenderness when he continued. "I'm sure that's not what he meant."

"Mom said, 'You don't mean that. Darcy is gifted in her own ways.' But the more she protested, the more Dad dug in. He got angry at her because she wouldn't admit what was so obvious to him. He said he'd lost his best hope, the only one who could achieve greatness. The smart one. The *better* one."

"Oh, sweetheart." Logan reached in to hug her, but she squirmed out of his arms.

"Don't. It's fine." She stood and walked away. "The point is, I know who I am. And who I'm not. Even my father could tell I'm not special." She turned, arms crossed, defiant. "I tried to prove him wrong, you know? I did my very best in school and achieved decent grades, but my test scores were barely above average. Dad went to Princeton. I got into NYU, and I think only because Dad pulled strings. I thought I might go to law school—Dana wanted to be a lawyer, you know?—but Dad told me I wouldn't be able to hack it. Of course he was right. I wouldn't have even gotten the publicist job if MJ hadn't recommended me. And what does my job matter? If I quit tomorrow, everybody's social media feed would be less cluttered. What do I really add to the world?"

Logan's lips were pressed tight, clearly fighting words he wanted to let fly. And then he pushed himself up, crossed the room, and pulled her into his arms. "Darcy."

"Don't." But she couldn't bring herself to push him away. He smelled of forest and musty clothes and something uniquely Logan. She'd missed that scent. She longed to hide in his arms and believe all his lies.

He leaned down and spoke into her ear. "You add *you* to the world. You're a beautiful gift. A treasure." He backed away to look at her. "I'm sorry your father is an idiot. He obviously has all the brains of a sweet potato, and I hate that you heard something so...stupid and ridiculous and obviously wrong when you were a child, too young to think it through logically. Your father was grieving."

"He's not grieving anymore, but his opinion of me hasn't changed a bit."

"Then he's a fool. But that's not your problem. Your father doesn't get to decide your worth."

"I know, I know." She'd heard this a million times from MJ. "I'm as valuable as I think I am."

"No." Logan's lips slipped into a smirk. "That's not true. Your value can't be changed because of anybody's opinion of you, not even yours, whether that opinion is good or bad. You're as valuable as *God* says you are. And God says you're so valuable that He died for you."

"Pfft." His words did nothing but raise her ire. "Jesus died for everyone, not just me. He died for the world."

"He's the Savior who left the ninety-nine to find the one," Logan said. "You are the one, Darcy, and He loves you."

"Everyone's 'the one.'" She pushed against his chest until he let her walk away.

"Because others are loved"—he spoke to her back—"does that make your being loved less special?"

Loved? Was she loved? Had she ever been truly loved for who she was, even though she wasn't special? Even though she wasn't gifted?

Her parents might not have divorced, but Daddy had checked out of the family after Dana's death. He'd spent all the years since pursuing money and power and, if rumors were to be believed, other women. No matter how hard Darcy tried—to prove herself, to get his attention, to achieve something worthwhile—Dad had never been impressed. He didn't even pretend to love her.

Since Darcy graduated from high school, even Mom's love had dwindled. Or maybe she'd just quit pretending. Lots of shopping excursions and phone chats about nothing that mattered. But Mom lived in Connecticut. She was busy with her life and her friends and her charitable causes. She had very little time for Darcy.

Even Logan's love had proved paltry. He'd left her too. If he'd ever really loved her, wouldn't he have come back to New

York? Or at least taken a moment to talk to her when she came to Shadow Cove for the funeral?

He hadn't. He'd barely looked at her.

If not for MJ, Darcy might not know love at all.

Logan reached for her, but she backed away. "I'm going to bed."

"Please, let's talk."

"There's nothing to talk about." She moved past him toward the door.

But he snatched her hand and held it. "Sweetheart."

"Don't call me that." She yanked her hand away, irrationally angry. Or maybe her reaction was perfectly rational, all things considered. "Don't stand there and tell me how important I am, not after you walked away from me and never looked back."

Just like everybody else.

CHAPTER THIRTEEN

Logan had spent more nights in this cabin than he could count, and he'd always slept like a baby.

Tonight, though, every time he closed his eyes, snatches of the day found him. Gunshots. The wrecked car. The feel of Darcy trembling beneath him as the man who hunted them searched just a few feet away.

And when he managed to stifle those thoughts, he heard Darcy's words again, her insane belief that she wasn't valuable.

And her anger that he'd left her—which she somehow added to the proof that she didn't matter.

He'd let her believe that. Not him alone, but he'd been a part of it. She'd always mattered to him. It was his fault she didn't know that.

That was something he would rectify, as soon as possible.

He had no idea what morning would bring. Whatever happened, he needed Darcy to know the truth. It was time to tell her everything.

Decision made, he finally drifted to sleep, only to be awakened by the sound of an engine rumbling nearby.

He stood, snatched his Ruger, and positioned himself just inside the cabin door.

The shooter was too close.

Logan had snuffed all the lights after Darcy fled into the bedroom. Between the darkness and the prickly hedge designed to hide the cabin, they should be safe.

Even so, he remained alert.

Within a few moments, the engine noise faded.

Breathing a prayer of thanks, Logan returned to the couch, this time leaving the pistol on the floor where he could reach it.

He drifted in and out of sleep until a different sound woke him, the soft snick of a latch. He peeked and watched Darcy cross from the bedroom to the door. She slipped outside.

Yawning, he sat up and stretched, then shoved his feet into his still-damp sneakers. When five minutes had passed and she hadn't returned, he grabbed his handgun and a flashlight and followed her into the moist, chilly air.

Stars twinkled overhead, but the moon had set, and a faint glow in the east told him dawn was coming. He stuck the flashlight in his pocket but held the gun in his hand, just in case.

The outhouse door was wide open.

"Darcy?" He kept his voice quiet, just in case.

No answer.

He rounded the cabin, calling her name every so often in case she'd eschewed the outhouse in favor of a secluded tree. But she wasn't within the hedge.

Stifling his frustration and worry, he slid through the opening in the prickly bushes and followed the trail.

He found her among the trees just a few feet from the edge of the pond, almost completely hidden.

He kept his voice soft. "What are you doing?"

She spun, gasping, and started to pull Dad's handgun from

her sweatshirt pocket. Fortunately, she realized who was there before she aimed.

He held his hands up like a bad guy in an old Western. "I surrender."

She dropped her arm. "You scared me."

"What are you doing out here? It's not safe."

"I was careful. I stayed out of sight."

"The shooter could be anywhere."

"But he's on that dirt bike. Didn't you hear him?" At his nod, she turned again to face the pond. "He drove away."

"Could've hiked back."

She lifted a shoulder and let it drop. "It felt safe."

Well, as long as she *felt* safe, that was what mattered.

He managed to keep the sarcastic remark to himself because, in the gray morning light, with the birds twittering their wake-up calls, a mist rising from the water, it did feel safe.

He hoped it wasn't an illusion as he stood beside her.

A white egret glowed against the dark water on the far shore, still as the rock where it perched.

"Thank you for sharing that stuff about your family last night," he said.

"I was tired."

Ah. Maybe she was embarrassed. "It's my turn to tell you a story."

"You don't owe me anything."

"I do, Darcy. We both know I do."

She swallowed but otherwise didn't react.

"Dad's stroke was bad," he said. "At first, he was practically helpless."

She sighed as if he'd wounded her. "I should've tried harder to understand why you had to leave college. I'm sorry for all the things I said to you. I was selfish. I knew your family wasn't wealthy, but I didn't really get it."

"How could you have? You'd never known want." He grinned, thinking of younger Darcy. "Remember when I told you I didn't have the money to take you to dinner, and you suggested we stop at the ATM?"

She dropped her face into her hands. "I was so dumb."

"Naive. And secure."

"Financially." She lifted her head, all amusement leached from her expression. "Which isn't the same as being secure like you were."

He considered her remark against the story she'd told the night before. The Partingtons were wealthy, but he'd been secure in his family's love.

He'd take his security over hers any day of the week.

"I'm sorry I repeated those stupid words last night," Darcy said.

He knew exactly what she meant—the knife she'd twisted. *It's not your job to save the world.*

"It was cruel of me back then," she added, "and cruel of me to repeat it."

"You didn't mean to use the same words, right? You didn't mean anything by it."

"Even so—"

"You apologized," he said. "I forgave you. Besides, your feet were killing you. I think you can blame a lot on aching feet."

She lifted one in front of her. "They're better today."

He hadn't noticed her footwear. She wore an old pair of waterproof boots, left at the cabin *just in case.*

"I hope it's okay."

"I'm glad you found them. Where were they?"

"Bottom of the trunk. I'll try not to damage them."

He chuckled. "Yeah, that's my biggest worry right now—boots no feet have worn for a decade."

She smiled up at him, holding his gaze a few seconds too long before turning back to the view.

The grays were taking on color, the stars flickering out.

"It's beautiful here." Her voice sounded reverent, as if they stood in a cathedral.

The view was nothing compared to the woman beside him. Her blond hair was rumpled and messy, her makeup long since worn off. To him, she was prettier now than when she'd been all put-together the day before. Her disheveled state reminded him of the carefree girl she'd been. The first time he'd laid eyes on her, she'd been lying flat on her stomach on the jetty in the harbor, reaching for something between the boulders, one bare foot sticking out to give her balance. She'd worn her trademark shorts and oversize sweatshirt, and when he ran to her—thinking she'd fallen and hurt herself—she looked at him and smiled. Even as a dumb kid, he'd been blown away by the power of that smile.

"Anyway." He needed to pick the story back up before he lost his nerve. "Dad's stroke was bad, but he recovered well. Within a couple of months, he was moving with a walker. He could talk and make himself understood. He could feed himself and take himself to the bathroom."

"I remember."

Even though their argument had erected a wall between them, they'd stayed in touch. They hadn't talked about their relationship or whether Logan would return to college, coming to an unspoken understanding that those conversations could wait until they were together.

Logan had kept her apprised of Dad's health and his work at the restaurant, which he managed while Mom stayed home to care for Dad. It'd been a challenge to get caught up on the ins and outs at first, but between everything Dad had taught him over the years and the head cook filling in the blanks, Logan had felt competent soon enough.

"Miles helped," he explained. "He was managing another restaurant in town, technically the competition, but he didn't care. I can't imagine what I would've done if he hadn't stepped in."

"I'm glad you had him." She sounded wistful. He'd had Miles. Who had Darcy relied on back then? After he'd left her, who had she confided in?

He'd been her best friend, and he'd left her alone. Dealing with the restaurant and his dad's stroke were hard, but he'd been surrounded by family.

Why hadn't he realized how painful his leaving must have been for her?

Rather than delve into that, he continued his story. "Dad was getting better. The more he was able to do, the more he resented Mom's staying home with him. Since he couldn't work, he wanted to take over the kids' schooling to give her a break. He could do that, but she was afraid to leave him alone with the little ones. He used to grumble about it—how she was mollycoddling him, how he was a grown man and didn't need babysitters. After weeks of that, Mom agreed to run some errands in town while Jewel stayed home and kept an eye on him. He did great.

"After that, she left him alone about once a week. Since there were no problems, Dad thought he didn't need anyone watching him anymore. At all. He pushed and prodded until, finally, Mom told me it was my turn for a break. She worked at the restaurant so I could take a day off." Logan's empty stomach churned. "I should have stayed at the house that day."

Darcy's head tipped to one side. "Where'd you go?"

"That was the day he fell." He avoided Darcy's question. "I wasn't there. By the time Jewel found him, it was too late."

Though Logan hadn't seen his father on the bathroom floor, he'd cleaned up the blood. Dad had fallen and cracked his skull. The coroner said the end had come quickly—probably within two or three minutes. Maybe Logan couldn't have changed the outcome. But maybe, if he'd been there, he could've gotten help in time.

Instead, his little sister, only thirteen at the time, had found their father's body. She'd blamed herself.

Mom had been at the restaurant, and she'd blamed herself.

But Logan was the one who'd gone so far away. He'd let his father talk him into it, even though he'd known, deep down, that Dad wasn't ready to be alone for so many hours straight.

Darcy's hand slid around his forearm. Her fingers were chilled, but the gentle pressure comforted him. "It wasn't your fault."

Logan didn't know when he'd crossed his arms and closed his eyes. He opened them now, fighting the urge to shake off Darcy's touch. Not because he didn't like it but because he did. Too much.

"I should have been there."

"How would that have helped?"

"If I'd been there, I'd have lurked at the bathroom door. I always did, just in case. Jewel was busy with the younger kids, but I would've attended to him. I could've called 911. If nothing else, I'd have been there too..." He swallowed the words, knowing they'd be filled with emotion.

Dad had died alone on that cold tile floor.

"Where were you?" Darcy asked.

He took a breath, swallowing all the grief the story resurrected. This was the part he needed her to understand. Not an excuse for his terrible behavior, but at least a reason. "When I heard the news, I was walking across Washington Square Park."

She gasped. "You were... You were in New York?"

"I'd grabbed my phone to text you, to find out where you were, when I saw that I'd missed a call from Mom."

"Oh. Oh, Logan." Tears filled her eyes, and she wrapped her arms around him. "I'm so sorry. I had no idea."

He didn't hug her back. He didn't deserve her kindness or her comfort.

His feelings for Darcy hadn't changed. The trip to New York that day had been Dad's idea, but he hadn't understood his own frailty. Logan had known Dad wasn't ready. He'd known something bad *might* happen.

It had never occurred to him how bad it could be.

A life untouched by grief can't fathom it. A life untouched by death doesn't understand how near it hovers. One moment of distraction behind the wheel. One tumble at the top of a staircase. One innocent slip, and it could all be over.

Before that day, Logan hadn't understood that his secure life wasn't so secure. That everything could be taken away in an instant.

He'd been desperate to make things right with Darcy. So he'd given in to his father's pushing and cajoling, even joking like he was doing Dad a favor. *"Fine, I'll go to New York so you'll stop nagging me."*

He could still see his father's wide, slightly lopsided grin. *"Go get her back, son."*

Logan had set out on a five-hour drive to Manhattan. While he'd been driving away, Dad had weakened.

Fallen. And died.

"It wasn't your fault."

Logan's arms were stiff at his sides, but Darcy didn't let up her hug.

"It wasn't, Logan." She looked up at him, moisture on her cheeks and in her eyes. "Accidents happen. Even if you'd been there—"

"I might've seen that he was unsteady. I might've—"

"Your father was a grown man. And stubborn, if I remember correctly."

Logan couldn't help the smile even as tears pricked his eyes. "He was that."

"His life belonged to him. You don't know what would've happened if you'd been there. Do you blame your sister?"

"Of course not."

"It's just as ridiculous that you blame yourself. You didn't know what was going to happen any more than Jewel did. Any more than your mom did. Any more than your dad did. There's no way to know what would've happened if circumstances had been different. Isn't that part of the faith thing, believing that God knows what's best, even if you don't understand?"

He couldn't seem to make himself speak. Instead, he gave in to his need and wrapped his arms around her, thankful he'd finally told her the truth. Maybe, now that he had, she'd understand the rest.

They stood like that as the world brightened. Birds twittered. A low splash in the pond was probably a fish or a frog.

Life going on, all around. His own heart beat wildly. He'd told Darcy almost all of it. And she was still with him, as he'd always known she would be.

This was the reason he'd never told her everything, because he knew she'd understand and sympathize, and he hadn't felt he deserved her. Not her sympathy—and certainly not her love.

But a lot of time had passed since then. He'd accepted Dad's death and usually knew that, even if he'd stayed home, he probably couldn't have prevented it. Most of the time, he didn't blame himself, just wished he'd been there.

Dad had died alone, but he'd known how loved he was. He hadn't needed Logan to say goodbye on this side when he had Jesus to welcome him on the other.

Logan had come to accept all of that. And he'd come to accept that his own silence had destroyed what he could've had with Darcy.

What he still wanted with her.

The problems remained, though. She lived in New York, and he was right where he was supposed to be, in Shadow Cove with the family that depended on him.

He backed away enough to see her face. "I should've told you everything at the funeral. I didn't have words. I still blamed myself. I blamed our relationship, as if my love for you had caused his death."

"That doesn't make sense."

"I know that now. Grief isn't logical. It was years before I started to come to terms with it. I should've reached out then. I shouldn't have let you go. I've never stopped regretting that."

She backed out of his arms, wiping her eyes. "I understand why you didn't come back. But why didn't you explain?"

"I knew you'd feel like you needed to stick by me, even though all your dreams for me were dead. I couldn't get my degree. I couldn't live in Manhattan. I couldn't do any of the things we'd planned."

Her eyes narrowed. "What do you mean, *my dreams* for you? They were your dreams too."

"They weren't, Darce. I went to NYU because you did." He wiped moisture from her cheeks with his fingertips, loving her smooth skin, her beautiful green eyes, bright with tears. Loving everything about her, even a decade later.

And knowing it wasn't going to matter.

"I would have stayed in New York because that was where you wanted to be. Whatever you dreamed, that was what I wanted for you. For us. But after Dad died, I couldn't pretend anymore."

"Pretend?" He didn't miss the hurt in her expression. "Was that what it was?"

"My feelings for you were a hundred percent genuine. But the rest of it…"

"Why? Why not tell me the truth?"

"I would have done anything for you."

He watched emotions flick across her face. Irritation. Anger. Then acceptance. And affection.

"I'm sorry," he said. "I should've told you all of this a long time ago."

"I wish you had."

He faced the water again but couldn't help taking Darcy's hand. "I had to stay here with my family. Your life was—and still is—in New York. I'm where I belong, and so are you. Even if Dad hadn't died, even if I hadn't had to leave school… I don't know if I could've stayed in New York. I was never happy there like you were."

He glanced her way to see her watching him still. She didn't say anything, but by the tightness of her lips, the way they turned down at the corners, she was thinking pretty hard about something.

"Was I?"

He tried to remember what he'd said. "Were you…what?"

"Happy there. You seem so sure."

"Weren't you? Aren't you?"

She turned and stared across the water.

He followed her gaze to the egret, still perched on the distant rock.

"You remember when we used to go to the library?" she asked.

She could spend hours among the shelves at the little house-turned-library in downtown Shadow Cove. The town had built a new library closer to the schools, all modern and shiny, the scent of musty old books nearly nonexistent. But the old one, with the worn green carpet, the ancient plumbing, the furnace that defied the librarian's demands for quiet...

For years after he'd returned to Shadow Cove, he'd walk to the library, just a block from the restaurant, to feel Darcy's presence. It was as if she were right there, around the corner, just out of reach.

She'd treated the university library, with its cold, echoing foyer, like her sanctuary, going there any time she had a free moment or needed to think.

He bumped her shoulder. "I could pretend to like the city, but pretending to like the library—that was a bridge too far."

Her smile was slight. "You were a good boyfriend."

He wasn't sure what to say to that.

"You want to know what my deep down, secret, never-tell-a-soul dream was?"

He turned to face her, confusion turning to a knowledge that felt so obvious, he couldn't believe he'd never seen it before. "You wanted to be a librarian."

Her eyes popped wide. "How did you—?"

"Lucky guess. Isn't there a degree in it? Library science or something?"

"There is." She looked at the lake again. "When I told Dad, he laughed. He said that it was just like me to want to take a job where my best friends would be books. Where I could hide behind a desk and tell customers about people who'd actually done something with their lives."

A flash of rage had Logan stifling a curse that he might just let fly if he ever saw Mr. Partington again.

"I don't know why I cared what he thought."

"I don't either." Logan tugged her hand until she faced him, needing her to hear him. "I don't know what your father's problem is, but he obviously doesn't know you at all. He doesn't see the woman I see. You're smart and talented and so..." And then another question occurred to him. "When you were young, you said you wanted to be in publishing—and you felt like you had to do that in New York, where the big publishers are located."

But librarians could live anywhere there was a library. He didn't dare speak the last part, afraid to put his hope into words.

"Publishing seemed like a good second choice from what I really wanted. But, being back here"—she looked around and laughed—"well, not here, certainly not under these circumstances, but back in Shadow Cove. I was never happier than when I was here." Uncertainty filled her eyes. He watched a war going on there, unsure what she was thinking. He hoped, though, hoped maybe...

"I was never happier than when I was with you."

Her words were a balm or a lifeline or...or some better metaphor he couldn't think of. All he knew was that, after all their years apart, they were together again. And even if the circumstances were all wrong, having her at his side was right in every sense of the word.

He rested his hands on her hips, giving her the opportunity to back away. He feared her next words would be that he'd misunderstood. That this wasn't what she wanted.

But she didn't say anything as her gaze flicked from his eyes to his mouth.

And that was it.

He lowered to meet her, pressing his lips against hers, telling himself to move slowly. To be gentle. But his body had different ideas.

He wrapped her in his arms and deepened the kiss.

Her hands slid around his neck, her fingers in his hair.

She was everything he'd missed and longed for and been certain he'd never have again. The world fell away until it was just Darcy and Logan, together again, as if nothing had changed.

As if nothing could come between them. Nothing could hurt them.

He trailed kisses down her neck, wanting more of her, more of this.

Her soft moan had him nearly exploding with desire.

He had to stop, even if it killed him.

He stood straight, crushing Darcy to his chest, unwilling to let her go.

"Logan."

His name was spoken on an exhale as if she fought to catch her breath the same way he did.

"I'm not sure... I don't know what you're feeling or thinking." His voice was rough. He backed away the slightest bit, needing to see her face. "Darcy, not a single day has gone by that I haven't thought about you. I know it sounds crazy, and I'm a jerk for not saying this to you sooner. I should've reached out years ago. I should've..." No, he wasn't going to let himself replay all the stupid mistakes he'd made. The past was the past.

Maybe, maybe they could have a future.

"I love you, Darcy." The pretending had been a band around his chest, tightening every year he didn't see her, every year he didn't make things right. Now, the band loosened. He could take a full breath again for the first time since his father's death. "If there's a chance for us—"

Across the pond, the egret took flight.

A faraway scream carried on the cool morning air.

CHAPTER FOURTEEN

Darcy had been lost in Logan's kiss. In his words. In his eyes.

The loud squawk of a bird had surprised her, but she hadn't been concerned.

The danger that'd followed them since the afternoon before had been so far from her mind.

By the time fear caught up, she was on the ground between a thick bush and the trunk of a tree, Logan's huge hands on her shoulders, keeping her down. "Don't move."

"But—"

"Stay here!" He ran toward the cabin, leaving her to put it together.

The high-pitched noise hadn't been a birdcall. It'd been MJ.

And now the man Darcy loved, loved more than her own life, was running to save her beloved aunt.

While she hid like a coward.

She took the handgun from her sweatshirt pocket and made sure the safety was off. She could defend herself, if she had to.

She peeked toward the trail leading to the cabin, but Logan

was gone. Within a few seconds, even the sounds of his running had faded. She was alone.

Seconds ticked into minutes while silence pressed in.

No more noises reached her.

No shouts, no screams, no rustling branches.

No birdcalls. No skittering creatures. No splashing fish. It was as if all the world waited with her.

Father, please!

Until the day before, she hadn't prayed in years, not because she didn't believe in Him but because...because He didn't believe in her. She'd never be good enough for God, just like she'd never been good enough for her own father. And facing either one of them just shined a spotlight on all the things she wasn't and could never be.

But this moment wasn't about her. It was about the two people she adored most in the world.

Please, protect them. Save them. Rescue them.

Maybe, if she didn't pray for herself, God would listen. Maybe, if she made it all about Logan and MJ, God would overlook all of Darcy's faults.

Please, God. Get them out of here. Get them away from that crazy person, whoever he is. Jonas? Or Xavier? Or...You know, Lord. Protect them.

She kept praying, kept begging as if He might be listening.

But she feared the silence was the only answer she was going to get.

Time dragged.

Slowly, the forest woke up. Birds chattered again. Squirrels hopped overhead, jiggling bushes and rustling leaves.

But Logan and MJ didn't come.

CHAPTER FIFTEEN

Logan feared he'd hurt MJ.

But if he had, that was a tiny thing. Nothing compared to his true terror.

That the man hunting them would catch their scent.

Logan held MJ's back against his chest, hand over her mouth to keep her from calling out.

He'd been running through the woods, parallel to the trail but far enough from it not to be seen. When he'd first caught sight of the older woman, she'd been barreling wildly downhill.

He'd angled and tackled her. Rolled her over and held her against himself, muffling her screams as he dragged her around a Volkswagen-sized boulder just off the path. "It's me," he'd whispered. "It's Logan. Stop fighting. It's me."

He'd had to repeat himself more than once. Finally, his words penetrated. She relaxed against him.

He strained to hear movement in the forest. But everything was still, as if all creation had paused to pray.

No sign of the hunter. Was he even here? Logan hadn't seen anybody but MJ, but the woman surely wouldn't have panicked without good reason.

A minute passed.

He whispered, his voice so quiet he could barely hear it. "I'm going to move my hand. You have to be quiet. Okay?"

She nodded, and he eased up his hold and pulled the handgun from his jacket pocket. If the shooter showed himself, Logan would be ready.

He was thankful for all the years of hunting and target practice with Dad. Even so, could he actually fire at a fellow human being?

It only took a second's thought to answer the question. If that human being was trying to kill the woman he loved—or someone she loved?

No question about it.

His mouth near MJ's ear, he whispered again. "You saw him?"

At the dip and rise of her chin, that was a yes.

"He saw you?"

Another nod had the acid that'd filled his stomach churning. His hands trembled. His heart raced. He felt on high alert—and unprepared.

Thank God he'd reached MJ before the shooter and had gotten her out of sight. But he'd left Darcy alone. It'd been instinct to hide her, an overwhelming desire to separate her from danger.

Now, he berated himself.

They should've stayed together.

An armed gunman was out here, somewhere. Probably waiting for them to show themselves.

What if Darcy got worried? What if she came looking for him and MJ?

She could be shot. She could be *killed.*

Keep her safe, Lord, please.

Logan had just gotten her back. The thought of losing her again was a red-hot poker to his heart.

With everything inside him, he wanted to go to her now. But he didn't dare move.

If this was a waiting game, Logan wasn't going to be the one to forfeit.

So he prayed silently, begging for guidance and rescue.

A rustling behind him had him turning.

At first, he saw nothing, and then something flashed—a glint on the far side of a tree a good fifty yards away. Then the shiny thing took shape—a rifle barrel.

"Down!" He shoved MJ flat and aimed at the masked man who poked his head out.

The gunman had to have seen him. He'd had plenty of time to shoot. Instead, he bolted in the other direction, running headlong into the forest.

He was too far away, and there were too many trees separating them, for Logan to get off a shot, though he thought about it.

But no.

He dropped the muzzle of the gun. He was not a shoot-a-man-in-the-back kind of guy, no matter what that man had done.

MJ sat up, watching where the shooter had disappeared. "Did you scare him away?"

Had he? With his Ruger? Good pistol, but not a hunting rifle like the gunman carried.

Had the guy even seen Logan's gun?

The shooter'd had the higher ground, the better weapon, and the element of surprise. Why run?

It didn't make sense.

Logan stood and held out his hand for MJ, his gaze on the

forest where the shooter had disappeared. There was no movement. The guy was gone—for now. "Let's get back to Darcy."

MJ took his hand, and he pulled her to her feet.

"Is she okay?"

"Was when I left her." He turned and crouched so MJ could climb on his back.

"Ankle's better. Or at least it was before I ran."

"Hop on." He wasn't up for a debate—or waiting while the older woman hobbled beside him. When she was on his back, he said, "Tuck in."

She did, and he moved as quickly as he could back to the opposite side of the trail toward the pond.

Why hadn't the gunman taken a shot? He'd been there before Logan had spotted him. He must've been creeping closer for a few minutes. If the guy hadn't made a noise, Logan wouldn't have known he was there.

He'd had plenty of time to take a shot. So...why hadn't he? Did he get cold feet?

It wasn't so easy to shoot a human being. Maybe the guy'd had second thoughts.

Or did he see Logan and MJ and realize he'd followed the wrong target?

That was the most logical explanation. Meaning the person after them wasn't stalking the famous psychologist-turned-celebrity at all.

He was after Darcy. Which meant...

Jonas.

As the name resounded in his mind, Logan picked up speed, desperate to get back to her before her psychopathic ex-boyfriend found her.

CHAPTER SIXTEEN

D arcy didn't know what to do.

Should she look for Logan and MJ or stay put?

What if they never came back? How long should she hide before she gave up? And when she gave up—if they never came —then what?

On her way out of the cabin, she'd grabbed the handgun Logan had given her the night before. And her phone, useless except for the flashlight. Maybe, she could creep down the mountain to the highway and stop a passerby. It would probably take hours, but if they never came back, if she had no other choice...

How could she leave Logan and MJ? She couldn't. But maybe they needed help. Maybe the best way to help would be to call the police?

What should I do?

Rustling noises, and then Logan stepped into view, MJ on his back.

They were safe. *Thank You, God.*

Logan looked as relieved as she felt.

MJ slid to her feet. "Are you all right?"

"I am. Are you?" Darcy searched her aunt's face as if trauma might be written there. "What happened?"

"No time for that." Crouching, Logan gave Darcy a long look. "Did you see anyone?"

"No. Did you?"

He didn't answer, just turned to MJ. "You said your ankle's better?"

"Yes." To prove it, she lifted the leg of the too-long sweatpants she'd changed into the night before. The swelling had gone down considerably. "Even after running, I think it's okay."

"He found the cabin?" Logan asked.

MJ nodded. "I don't know how."

Darcy hadn't considered what must have been obvious to Logan, that their only refuge was gone. At the thought of trail mix and bottled water they'd left behind, she wanted to cry.

Ridiculous to be so sad about that, but she was hungry and scared and...

And someone was trying to kill them.

MJ continued. "I was in the outhouse when—"

"You can tell us after. There's a cave not too far from here. We're going to have to get there, which'll involve some climbing. Can you do it?"

MJ squared her shoulders. "I can."

When Logan looked at Darcy, she said, "No problem."

He stood and peered into the forest all around. Finally, he held out a hand to help Darcy up. "Let's go."

She stood and nodded for MJ to follow Logan.

Darcy moved behind her aunt, staying close. Now that she had these two back, she wasn't about to be separated from them again.

~

Some climbing.

That was what Logan had said.

Darcy had followed him and MJ about halfway down the hill they'd ascended the night before, and then Logan took a sharp turn. They picked their way past boulders and among trees, stopping at the edge of the world.

Or so it felt as the forest gave way to air and space. And a cliff.

When Darcy and her aunt stood at his side, he pointed at a shadow. "There it is."

"Uh…" MJ leaned forward as if that would help.

The sun was still low on the horizon. Darcy strained to see what Logan saw but gave up after a few seconds.

"Trust me," he said. "There's a cave there. I'm going first. MJ, you come right behind. Put your hands and feet where I do." He faced Darcy. "Keep your eyes on your aunt and do what she does. We have to move quickly—"

"I get it." If the gunman saw them when they were on the rock wall, they'd be as easy to pick off as targets in a carnival game.

"Whatever you do," Logan said, "don't look down." He shoved his feet onto an outcropping, grabbed handholds just a little over his head—low enough for Darcy and MJ to reach—and shimmied sideways toward the cave very few people knew existed.

This was insane.

But if they could get there, they'd be safe. How could anybody else find it? And even if the shooter did, he couldn't reach it without being seen.

MJ went next, mimicking Logan's movements.

The wall wasn't vertical, as Darcy had originally thought. Even so, a fall from here…

She did exactly what she wasn't supposed to do.

She looked down.

She'd seen this cliff from the bottom the night before, but it hadn't seemed nearly so high. She wasn't great at judging distances. Was it thirty feet high? Forty? A few bushes grew on thin soil along the steep slope, but if somebody fell, they'd probably slide right past those.

At the bottom, the little stream looked no wider than a snake as it meandered past a jagged rock formation at the base of the cliff.

What would it feel like to fall, to hit those rocks? The damage would be extensive, the pain excruciating, assuming a person survived…

"Darcy."

Logan's hiss had her shaking herself out of the morbid thoughts.

Logan was in the cave already. He helped MJ inside and then lowered his feet toward the ledge. "I'll come back."

"No." She tried to match her volume to his. "I got it." She didn't want him to risk his life again because she'd been distracted by fear.

She lifted one foot onto the wall, the man-sized boots she'd donned feeling unsteady on the small ledge, especially with her feet moving around inside them. She found places to dig her fingers in and then, after a breath of prayer, brought the other foot off solid ground.

She held there a moment, breathing.

And then she climbed, inching upward and to the right, toward Logan. She didn't dare look to see how much space separated her from the cave. Didn't dare look down. She moved steadily, one step, one handhold at a time.

It wasn't as far as it'd seemed from the forest. And it wasn't as steep.

Within a few minutes, the ledge beneath her feet widened.

But a noise sounded from below, a loud snap.

"Hurry!" Logan hissed. "I see him down there!"

Adrenaline flooded her veins and made her hands tremble. She shoved her fingers into a hole in the stone.

She slipped and tipped to one side.

Fighting for balance, she glimpsed the ground below, the jagged stones reaching up, beckoning her toward them.

No.

She held a tiny handhold and pressed her body into the rocks. Her heart pounded, her blood rushing in her veins.

She could feel Logan's terror as he watched from a few feet away. "Come on, Darce. You can do this."

Wasn't like she had a choice.

Steady again, she inched, inched toward him.

As soon as he could reach her, he grabbed her upper arms.

She pushed off the ledge and propelled herself into the small cave with such force that she barreled against him.

His arms came around her as he tumbled onto his back, letting out a low, "Oomph."

"I'm sorry." Darcy landed on his chest and immediately tried to scramble away. But he didn't let up his hold. "I didn't mean..."

Her words trailed at his chuckle. "If you need a hug, you only have to ask."

Joking? He was joking? Now? She couldn't match the humor in his voice. "Did I hurt you?"

His face was almost impossible to make out in the darkness. "That was terrifying."

"You looked like you'd done it a million times."

"Not *my* climb." He still didn't let her go. "Watching you. Pure torture."

"I was that bad, huh?" What was wrong with her voice? With Logan so close, so very *there...*

"Your every move…" His voice trailed. He pushed her hair away from her face. "Thank God you made it."

Before she could come up with a suitable response—and her mind was too muddled with adrenaline and Logan to think of words—he weaved his fingers into her hair and drew her close.

He crushed her lips to his, and all the terror of the moment morphed and shifted.

As much as she'd feared that climb, she loved being in his arms. She poured herself into him, poured all her feelings into the moment, feeling safe and protected and…

Oh, yes.

"Well, that explains where you two went this morning."

MJ's voice had Darcy breaking the kiss and lifting her head, embarrassed and confused. What was she doing, making out with Logan like they were teenagers out for a hike?

Logan chuckled again, and she felt his amusement—or was it relief?

It was all too much. She was terrified of the gunman tracking them like prey. She was desperate to get off this mountain, to get to help. And a shower. And a meal.

All that was true.

Even so, being in Logan's arms felt perfect.

CHAPTER SEVENTEEN

L ogan had to pull himself together.

He'd experienced Darcy's death a thousand times in the few minutes it took her to get from the ground to the cave. His relief at having her safe had turned to something else when she landed in his arms.

He sat up and moved past Darcy so he could look outside. And put distance between them, needing space from all the temptation Darcy was to him. He crouched beside MJ. "Any sign of him?"

The fear in the older woman's expression said enough.

Logan spotted the man. Standing behind a bush near the base of the cliff, he was dressed in black jeans and an army-green camo jacket. A ski mask covered his face, but he seemed to be scanning the cliff wall. His rifle barrel glinted in the morning sunshine.

Darcy perched behind him and looked over his shoulder.

"Back up, both of you." Logan kept his voice steady. "Behind me."

"You too," Darcy said. "He could shoot you too."

"Nobody's getting shot." Logan urged the women deeper into the cave.

MJ sat against the wall across from Darcy. They were so close that MJ's feet were nestled against Darcy's hips—and vice versa.

The ceiling was low enough that he had to crawl to avoid bumping his head.

"You think he knows where we are?" Darcy asked.

Logan settled with his back to the wall beside her, stretching as much as his long legs would allow. He stayed close to the opening, watching outside. "I'd guess he knows enough." Logan glanced at Darcy but could barely make out her features in the darkness. "As long as we can see him, we know where he is." To MJ, he said, "What happened back at the cabin? Were you looking for us?"

"No. I hadn't been awake enough to know you were gone. I went to the outhouse, and when I came out, I saw him peeking in one of the windows."

"How did he not hear you?"

"I saw him before I let the door close. I crept around the cabin looking for the opening in the hedge. I was almost through when I heard him coming."

"Did he say anything?"

"No, but he was running. He must've seen me. I pushed through and screamed and ran. I was trying to get away, but the woods were so thick that I couldn't move fast enough. So I ran back toward the path. And then you tackled me."

Darcy reached for MJ's hand. "That must've been terrifying. Thank God you got away." She grabbed Logan's hand too. "Thank God you got to her."

Logan imagined the scene MJ painted. "I didn't see him. You're sure he was behind you?"

"Yes. I heard him." Her voice bordered on defensive.

"I believe you." If she got through the hedge but he didn't see the opening, it might've taken him a few moments to follow her out of the cabin's yard. "When you were in the woods, which side of the path were you on?"

"The same side where we hid. Why?"

"He was behind us."

Darcy gasped.

"What?" MJ's eyes were wide with fear. "Is that why you pushed me down? I didn't realize... He was right there?"

"Close enough to shoot. But he didn't." Which Logan still couldn't understand. He'd had them. He'd seen them, no doubt about it. "I was thinking maybe he had second thoughts, but"—he looked outside—"he's still there. Still tracking us. So if he did—"

"What does it mean?" MJ asked.

"It means we're trapped." Darcy pulled her hands back and crossed her arms, though from cold or fear, Logan wasn't sure.

"At least we can defend ourselves." He pulled out the Ruger. If the man came close, Logan would be ready.

"Do you think you could hit him from here?" MJ asked.

He considered the question. "Maybe. But I won't shoot unless he shoots first."

"How deep does the cave go?" Darcy asked.

"Deep," Logan said. "When I was a teenager, I was up here with Dad, Miles, and Miles's daughter. Linny and I crept all the way to the end. Back then, there was a little opening near the pond."

"An opening?" MJ started to move. "Let's go find it."

"Hold up," he said. "Someone has to stay and watch. Can you shoot?"

The older woman nodded. "I grew up in Maine too."

"Good. With your ankle, I think you should stay here. Darce, you want to stay or come with me?"

"I'll come."

"Then give her your handgun."

Darcy did, and MJ took it and checked the chamber like a pro. "What do I do if he leaves?"

"It's not that big a cave. We'll hear if you call. I don't think he's going anywhere. I'm pretty sure he saw Darcy."

He watched Darcy's face as he delivered that news. It was hard to see in the dim light, but her back stiffened. "Why do you think that?"

"I saw movement in the forest behind you. I think he caught sight of you, but by the time he reached the cliff edge, you'd disappeared. Unless he's spent a lot of time in these woods, he can't know about the cave, but he knows we're around here somewhere. He's not going to give us the chance to escape." He focused on the older woman. "Stay out of sight and keep watch. If he leaves, let us know right away."

"Will do," MJ said. "You two be careful."

Logan pulled out his flashlight and flicked it on, then crawled over MJ and Darcy toward the back of the cave.

On hands and knees, Logan crept into a tunnel that got narrower as they went. The way was smooth. He was pretty sure the stream used to flow this way, which would explain the polished floor. Thank God he'd grabbed his flashlight, or they'd be in total darkness.

"You really think we'll hear MJ if she calls?" Darcy's voice seemed to boom in the tiny space.

"We could test it, but I'm afraid your friend would hear us."

"Not my friend."

"Hmm."

"What? What do you mean, hmm?"

He should really keep his mouth shut. "It's tight here." He dropped to his stomach and army-crawled forward.

"I don't like this. What happens if we get lost and can't get back to MJ?"

"There's one way in and one way out." He was pretty sure, anyway. "The cave's not that big. You can wait there if you want."

She didn't respond, and he couldn't look behind to see if she followed.

Up ahead, the flashlight beam, which had bounced off the cave walls, suddenly seemed to get lost in a void. He scrambled forward and out of the tunnel into a small opening.

She gasped, the sound echoing.

"Are you coming? Can you see the light?"

"I hate this." But a moment later, she crawled out of the tunnel and stood beside him. "Wow."

"It's smaller than I remember." He shifted the flashlight around the cavern.

Cavern was a big word for such a small space. Logan raised his hand over his head and touched the ceiling. The room was oblong, probably six feet wide, maybe ten deep.

He breathed in fresh air. "Smell that?"

She inhaled. "What am I...smelling for?"

"It's not stale. Meaning there's got to be an opening somewhere."

"You don't know where?"

"It's been twenty years. It must be overgrown." He moved the beam more slowly across the ceiling, but the lack of daylight didn't bode well.

He walked around, aiming the flashlight up and pushing on the stone like there might be a secret door to Narnia or...Middle Earth.

"Why did you call the shooter *my* friend? The way you said it made me think you know something you haven't told me."

He hated to think how she'd take this, but he couldn't put it off any longer. He didn't pause in his search. "The gunman had us. He was behind us, fifty yards away, no more. That's a long distance with a handgun, but he's got a rifle. If he has any skill with the thing at all—and the fact that he hit a moving car yesterday tells me he does—then he could've picked me off before I even knew he was there. He could've shot me and MJ."

"So close?"

"The point is, he didn't shoot. We already know he's not after me. The fact that he didn't even try to take a shot at your aunt..." Logan crossed the middle of the space and stood in front of Darcy, wanting to see her reaction to his hypothesis. "I think he's after you."

"Jonas." The single word held terror.

"I can't see any other reason why he wouldn't have shot at me and your aunt."

"But I don't... It doesn't make sense. He blames me for the promotion he didn't get, but could he really hate me enough to kill me? I mean... He said he loved me. How does that happen?"

"What's that old expression? A fine line between love and hate? And with a psychopath—"

"He's not a psychopath."

"I'm sorry, but I think he is." Logan told her about Jonas's plot to have him not only kicked out of school but arrested. Though it was too dark to make out the look on her face—he'd aimed the flashlight at the floor to keep from blinding her—he could feel her horror as he related the story.

"Why didn't you tell me?" Her words were barely more than a whisper.

"The girl asked me not to. I shouldn't have agreed. If I'd told you, you wouldn't have started dating him in the first place."

"But Jonas thinks you're the reason I turned down his proposal. Not saying he should want to kill you, but if he's willing to kill me, why not you?"

"I'm guessing he didn't recognize me. It has been a decade, and he hasn't gotten a good look at me. Does he know I'm from Maine?"

"I don't know. I doubt it. If what you're saying is true, then this really is my fault."

"Don't do that again." Logan resumed his search for the opening. It had to be here somewhere. "There's no way you could've known what he was capable of, and that's my fault. But at the end of the day, if Jonas is trying to kill you... That's his fault."

Logan hadn't even gone hunting since his dad's death. Much as he liked the taste of venison, he took no pleasure in ending the life of any creature.

But if it came down to a choice between Darcy and Jonas...

Logan would take the man out.

CHAPTER EIGHTEEN

Darcy hovered near the tunnel that would take them back to MJ, worried that if she didn't, they might not be able to find the small opening again. The floor angled downward toward her as if this were a basin, the tunnel a drain.

Meanwhile Logan prowled the tiny space of the second cavern, his hands skimming along the ceiling. He'd started where the ceiling met the walls and was slowly moving in a spiral pattern toward the center.

All she saw was rock. As far as she could tell, there was no way out.

"Got it," Logan said.

"Got what?" Not until she was right beside Logan did she see what he saw—a break in the otherwise smooth ceiling, a crease. Not an opening, though. Just more rocks.

"Come here." Logan tugged her closer. "Lift your hand here."

She did, opening her palm as if in worship.

"You feel that?"

Now that he mentioned it, the slightest breeze skimmed across her skin.

"Step back," he said. "Let me see if I can open it up."

She moved out of the way, and Logan shoved his fingers into the small opening. He dug and shifted and then tossed something against the far wall. She couldn't see in the darkness but guessed, based on the thud, that it was a rock.

Another followed.

And another. Minutes passed while she watched, praying silently.

She'd prayed more in the previous twenty-four hours than she had in years. In New York, among the high-rises and powerful people, God felt distant and distracted. But here, in the woods, in a cave—in need—He felt close again, like He had when she was a child.

Did God prefer Maine to New York? She doubted that. No, it wasn't that He wasn't in New York. It was that she hadn't been looking for Him there. She certainly hadn't believed she'd find Him.

But He was here. Even in the dark, dank cave, she could feel His presence.

And then she saw the most beautiful sight she could imagine.

Pale light streamed in through the hole.

Logan spun and grinned. "We got it."

She started toward him, but he held up a hand. "Just in case."

Suddenly she imagined rocks falling and crushing him. "Be careful!"

His laugh did something to her insides. How had she lived apart from this man for ten years? Just being in his presence made her feel alive again.

"The biggest danger is getting covered in dirt."

She saw what he meant as pebbles and soil rained down. The opening got larger, not a hole so much as a space between two giant boulders, one angled atop the other, leaving a small gap.

He kept working a few more minutes, grunting, pushing, pulling. He paused to catch his breath. Then he started pushing again, trying to shift a rock wedged in the gap. They could only see one side of it, but the way it held fast told her it was a lot larger than it seemed from their vantage point. Also, she suspected it was the reason the two larger rock-plates weren't touching. If he succeeded in moving the one he was pushing, would it open the gap wider, or close it completely?

"Wait." She bumped his hip. "Move out of the way a sec."

He did, and she gazed through the opening, which gave only a tiny glimpse outside. Ground, brush, and the trunk of a tall pine tree. "I think I can get through that. Don't you?"

"I can't," Logan said.

"Right. But I can go—"

"No."

"I'm sure of it," she said. "Boost me up."

"No."

Oh. He wasn't arguing that she wouldn't fit. He was refusing to let her go.

She stepped back and stuck her hands on her hips. "Why not?"

"He's trying to kill you."

She pointed at the tunnel. "He's way over there."

"It's not that far, Darce. He could see you."

"How?"

"We're at the edge of the hill. If you went the wrong way—"

"So tell me the right way."

"No."

"Logan."

"Go back and sit with your aunt. I'll keep working on this." He piled all the debris he'd pulled into the cave under the opening, then climbed on top. It gave him about three inches of height, which wasn't going to improve his angle or give him enough torque to shift a boulder.

"You're trying to move a mountain," Darcy said.

"My God moves mountains."

Right. But from where she stood, the mountain seemed pretty intent on staying right where it was.

"Do you have a crane I'm not aware of?"

"Go sit with MJ. She's probably worried."

"Listen to me."

He stepped off the dirt and crossed his arms, definitely not the posture of someone open to having his mind changed.

"If it is Jonas—"

"Then he's trying to kill you. And you want me to just let you—"

"First of all, you don't *let me* do anything."

"Good luck getting out without my help."

She glared, though he wasn't wrong. "Second of all, if it is Jonas, then he doesn't know these woods like you do. He doesn't know where the cave is, and he definitely doesn't know there's another exit."

If anything, Logan's expression turned darker. Probably because he knew where her thoughts were taking her.

"MJ hasn't called out to us, so that means he's still there, watching the entrance."

"But he could see—"

"If I duck and you tell me where to go, then I can get away without him seeing me. Right?"

"It's too dangerous."

"Is it possible, Logan?" She already knew the answer. If they couldn't get out this way without Jonas—or whoever it was—seeing them, then why bother finding this exit in the first place? Obviously, Logan had believed escape through here was possible—until he realized only she'd be able to use it.

His head dipped the slightest bit, a silent affirmation.

"As long as he's still at the bottom of the cliff, I can go. I can run to the highway and flag someone down."

"No."

"Stop that. You're being obstinate."

"I'm trying to protect—"

"I get it. If you think it's your job to protect me and MJ, fine. I get it. I think it's my job to protect the two of you. And if MJ had a chance to do the protecting, I'm sure she'd jump at it. You don't have to do it alone. You're not Superman. Neither one of us is Lois Lane."

"You are not going out there—"

"It's not your job to save the world, Logan."

He scowled at the familiar words. "Jonas. Wants. You. Dead."

"Even if it's him"—she pointed up at the small exit—"he isn't there."

"No."

"So we'll just wait here until he finds a way to get to us. Or the sun goes down and we don't see him coming. Just wait for him to come and kill us."

"We'll wait for help."

"How long will that be, Logan? How long—?"

"I don't know! I can't..."

She understood his fear. She did.

"No." He turned away. But the word didn't carry the finality of his previous refusals. It held a hint of...possibility.

So she waited.

"The highway is too far," he said. "We're only about a mile from the retreat center."

"What? How can that be?"

"It's a mountain." He turned back to face her, exhaling his frustration. "The retreat center is near the top. We walked around the side last night, then climbed. I don't know exactly where it is from here, but I don't think it would be hard to find."

"Okay, then. Let me go."

He started working the opening again, yanking and pulling, grunting when dirt fell into his face.

His arms dropped to his sides. He stared up through the gap for a long, long time, the dim light illuminating his fear. His eyes squeezed closed, his mouth pinched shut.

Then, he lowered his gaze to hers. "I can't lose you, Darcy. I just got you back, and I can't lose you."

His tender words had her feet moving toward him. She wrapped her arms around him and rested her cheek on his sweatshirt. "I feel the same. It's like...like this thing we've found —you and me—is the most delicate blown glass, and if we let it slip at all, it'll shatter."

He held her against his chest. She could feel his relief, as if she'd agreed to stay with him. Not just later but right now.

"If it's real, Logan... If it's meant to be, then nothing will break it."

"You're not a metaphor." His words were vehement. "You're flesh and blood—and breakable."

"But Jonas-or-whoever is watching the entrance. He won't see me. I'll run for help. It's the only—"

"We could send MJ. She would fit."

Darcy backed out of his arms. "You'd send a woman with a sprained ankle—"

"Let's ask her and see what she says." Suddenly, he looked confident, and she guessed why.

MJ wouldn't put Darcy in danger. No matter how much pain she was in, she'd want to go herself. Which was ridiculous.

But if Darcy was going to argue her case, she might as well argue it to both of them at the same time.

Logan followed Darcy back through the tunnel, growing more determined by the foot.

He hadn't brought them this far, protected them this long, to let Darcy run into danger now.

There had to be a better way. *Lord, what should I do?*

As soon as Darcy reached the opening near the mouth of the cave, MJ asked, "What'd you find?"

Darcy scooted forward and sat across from her. "Logan was right. There is another way out, but it's only wide enough for me to get through."

"Or you, MJ." Ignoring Darcy's glare, he crawled forward and peeked outside. "He still there?"

"He lit a campfire."

Sure enough, the scent of burning wood carried on the breeze along with...bacon?

He'd always known Jonas had a cruel streak. Cooking bacon close enough that they could smell it? Torture technique, no question. "I don't see him." Logan settled beside MJ—away from Darcy and her distracting presence and her stupid plan.

"About a yard to the right of that birch," MJ said. "You can see his jacket."

Sure enough, one shoulder of Jonas's camouflage jacket showed from behind the trunk of a wide oak just a couple of feet from where the smoke rose.

"He moves every so often but always ends up back there. He probably thinks his jacket makes him invisible. Tell me about the other way out."

"The opening is too small for me to fit through," he said, "but I think you could do it."

He was a heel for suggesting it. He wanted to protect both the women, but he couldn't figure another way out of this. If one was going to put herself in danger, he'd prefer it be MJ.

He knew she'd prefer that too. They both wanted to keep Darcy safe.

"I can do it," Darcy said.

He didn't even glance her way. "I think the man out there is after Darcy, not you."

MJ's eyes widened as she turned to her niece. "Why would anybody want to hurt you?"

"I'm not sure anybody does. Logan thinks it's Jonas."

He explained his reasoning, thinking MJ would agree with his conclusion, but she was shaking her head.

"I don't see it. Jonas is...off, I'll give you that." Again, she focused on Darcy. "I never liked him very much. I always thought he was...insincere."

"Why didn't you tell me that?"

"You knew him better than I did. I figured you knew what you were doing."

Darcy crossed her arms. "If I told you he'd asked me to marry him—?"

"I might've shared my opinions. I don't know." To Logan,

she said, "I'm just saying, yeah, the guy's insincere. But I don't think he's a killer."

"You just said you don't know him."

Darcy said, "I do, and I don't think—"

"We don't know." Logan didn't want to argue. "The point is, he might be after Darcy. If he was after you, then why didn't he take the shot when he had us in his sights?"

"Maybe he didn't want to hit you," MJ said.

Logan fought to keep his temper in check, but that theory didn't hold water. The man must be a killer. He'd shot at the car, hadn't he? Shot at both the women. Why would he care if a random stranger became collateral damage? No, Logan thought the man hadn't fired because his target hadn't been there.

And yeah, he could be wrong. It could be he was grasping for any excuse to keep Darcy with him, where she'd be safe.

Maybe MJ read his mind because she said, "Whoever it is, we need help. What do I have to do?"

"Climb to the retreat center. You said your ankle is better?"

"Yup." MJ sounded confident. "Just tell me what direction—"

"Wait." Darcy grabbed her aunt's hand but focused on Logan. "You're not seriously going to send my sixty-one-year-old—"

"Hey." MJ scowled at her. "No need to bring my age into this. I got this far, didn't I?"

"Logan carried you."

"I sprained my ankle." Her tone was defensive.

Darcy flipped her hand out, palm up. "Exactly. Not only are you *slightly* older than I am, but you're injured."

"It's better." MJ moved her foot in a circle, wincing.

Logan pretended not to notice. Yeah, the climb would be painful. But she could do it. To save Darcy—

"Is it well enough to climb a mile—or more?" Darcy gentled her voice. "Well enough to run if he sees you?"

"I ran this morning." But MJ's voice lacked certainty. She looked from Darcy to him. "Could we make the opening big enough for you to squeeze through?"

"Unfortunately, no."

"We have no food and no water," Darcy said. "If this turns into a waiting game, unless help comes soon, he wins."

"I can do it," MJ said. "I'll be fine."

She didn't sound at all confident.

He leaned his head back against the stone and closed his eyes. What kind of a jerk asks a woman her age to save him?

But it was MJ or Darcy.

Or they had to stay here and wait the guy out.

By now, somebody must have reported them missing. Miles was probably at the retreat center with a bunch of cops. They'd search. But how far, and how long would it take? Logan and the women had walked a couple of miles the night before. Would police assume they were still on the mountain? Or would they assume the three of them had been abducted? Or murdered, their bodies dumped?

There was a cheerful thought.

Miles knew about the cabin and the pond. Would he send searchers this way?

It was a matter of when.

If Miles didn't think to mention the cabin...as big as this mountain was, it might take days before help reached them. How long could they survive?

And what if Jonas came up with a way to smoke them out? Once it got dark, he could climb down from overhead or up from below or even attack from the side. Would they be able to see him? In time?

What should Logan do?

Send Darcy into danger, or wait for danger to find them?

Lord, there's got to be a way. Show me.

He listened, hard, hoping God would present door number three.

Please.

Darcy could climb out the hidden opening, move toward the top of the cliff where Jonas would see her, and lure him up there. If she could hurry back into the cave before he got there, then they could climb down the cliff.

Except Jonas would be able to see them from the top and the bottom—and even during his climb up through the woods if he stayed close to the cliff wall. Could they get away before he realized he'd been duped?

Maybe.

But Logan wouldn't count on it.

He opened his eyes to find MJ and Darcy watching him.

Darcy looked determined.

MJ looked fearful. He knew how she felt.

"We can literally see him," Darcy said. "As long as he's down there and I'm"—she pointed back and up—"out there, he's not going to come near me."

"You don't know these woods."

"Neither does he."

The argument surprised him because it came from MJ.

MJ, who was supposed to be on his side.

The older woman nudged Logan's shoulder. "I don't want her to do it, either. But it seems like the best way. This guy's been on our heels ever since that first gunshot. We finally have a way to outsmart him. I think we should take it."

"And risk Darcy's life?"

"She'll be farther from him than either of us, Logan." MJ pointed toward the mouth of the cave again. "Whether it's Jonas or somebody after me, he's right there. It'll be okay." She took Logan's hand and weaved their fingers together. "I love her too. We're going to have to cross our fingers and hope for the best."

Yeah. Because crossed fingers always made such a huge impact.

"The longer we wait," MJ added, "the better the chances are he figures out a way to get to us."

"What if he realizes what we're doing?" Logan pulled his hand away from MJ's. Regardless of her logic, he couldn't help seeing her as a traitor. "What if he catches up with her?"

"If he does," Darcy said, cutting her aunt off, "then he does." She looked at the sunny afternoon outside, rubbing her lips together. "At least you two will be—"

"Don't do that."

She cringed at his tone.

"That...that *my life is insignificant* stuff doesn't fly with me."

"Wait." MJ looked between them. "What are we talking about?"

Darcy kept her focus on Logan. "You don't own me."

"I don't own you. But I *love* you. With all my heart. You matter to me. You're *everything* to me. There's no chance I get behind your leaving this cave if you're going to have that...that stupid, cavalier attitude about your own safety."

Darcy blinked several times. Even in the dim light of the cave, he saw moisture in her eyes. Great. He'd made her cry.

"What is this?" MJ asked again. "What cavalier attitude?"

Logan glared at Darcy, daring her to tell her aunt the crazy things she'd said to him the night before.

When she didn't, Logan was tempted to, but now wasn't the time for a heart-to-heart about Darcy's worth. Besides, MJ would probably tell her to cross her fingers and believe in herself and appeal to the *god of me.*

Darcy needed Truth, not world-centric psychobabble.

She needs Truth? The words were a whisper in his heart. *What about what you believe?*

What about it? He knew God. He'd walked with Him all his life.

But do you trust Me?

He was tempted to brush the question off. He could do soul-searching later. But God didn't ask questions if they didn't matter.

Darcy's words—spoken three times now—came back to him. *It's not your job to save the world.*

Of course it wasn't. But he did have jobs to do. Like, it was his job to provide for his family.

Except...no. That was God's job. And if Logan messed it up, God would still be there. He'd provide.

It was Logan's job to protect Darcy and MJ. But...

He didn't want to say it. Didn't want to even think it. But... that was God's job too. God could handle their protection.

Open your hands, son. I've got this.

Logan's hands were clenched, literally and figuratively. He was afraid to surrender. What if God didn't provide? What if He didn't protect?

Did Logan really believe he could do a better job?

No, but he sure acted as if he did.

God could handle their protection. He'd brought them this far. Logan had to trust He would take them all the way to safety.

He stretched his hands and opened his eyes to find Darcy watching him.

"I'll do everything in my power to stay alive," she said. "I promise."

"I don't see another way," MJ added. "For all of our sakes, I think she should go for help."

Logan and Darcy had split up once already that day, and

he'd sworn he wouldn't do it again. Those minutes, wondering if she was safe or hurt, had nearly driven him mad.

How would he survive this?

But he could think of no better options. And God would be with her. He'd promised.

CHAPTER TWENTY

Sitting on the stone floor, Darcy memorized the directions Logan gave her back to the retreat center and the door code to get inside.

"Miles will probably be there," Logan said. "I'm guessing the woods will be crawling with police. They'll have found your rental and my van. You'll probably run into someone before you even get there."

"What if we just fired the handgun?" MJ suggested. "Wouldn't they hear?"

Darcy expected hope to light Logan's eyes, but he shook his head. "They might, but it would be faint. If they knew what it was, I'm not sure they'd be able to tell what direction it came from. I had trouble doing that yesterday after Jonas—"

"Or whoever," Darcy said.

"—shot at you, and I was just a quarter mile away. So, I'm not sure that would help."

"If they're out looking for us, though..." MJ's tone was less than hopeful.

"It might help," Logan said. "But we'd have to fire more than once. It seems wise to save our ammunition."

He was right. They'd loaded the handguns the night before but hadn't brought any extra bullets with them.

"Is that it?" Darcy asked. "Are we ready?"

He nodded but suddenly couldn't seem to speak.

MJ handed her gun to Darcy, gave her a fake smile, and squeezed her hand. "You'll do great."

"Sure." She matched her aunt's bravado. "I'll see you soon." She crawled forward and gave MJ an awkward hug, refusing to linger. She wouldn't consider that this might be her last chance to see this woman who'd meant so much to her.

This was Darcy's idea. She couldn't chicken out now.

But leaving them here, going into those woods by herself...

She couldn't let them see her fear.

Logan led the way. The tunnel seemed shorter. It didn't give her time to reconsider.

In front of her, Logan reached the cavern and stood. Daylight seeped through the opening, bathing the room in dim light.

She'd barely managed to get to her feet before he pulled her close. She reveled in his warmth and tenderness, the strength in his arms. The beating of his heart beneath her ear.

She'd had fun with teenage Logan, tall and lanky and happy. She'd been amazed by him in college, witnessing his work ethic as he focused on his classes.

She'd admired the son and brother she'd seen at his father's gravesite, selflessly supporting his family.

But this mature man was everything she'd always known he would be. Kind, gentle, and protective. And so much more.

She leaned back and slid a hand over his whiskers, prickly beneath her palm. "I love you, Logan Webb."

He made a noise in his throat, a groan stifled, and settled his forehead against hers. "Not a day has gone by that I haven't loved you. I'm sorry I didn't—"

"No more of that. We both made mistakes. We both said and did stupid things. Let's leave the past in the past."

"Yeah." He nodded. "Promise me you'll be safe. You'll do everything in your power to be safe."

"I promise I will. I've never had more to live for than I do right now."

He pulled her against his chest again. "Father, You are able to deliver Darcy. Let Jonas—or whoever that is out there—not harm her or anyone. Protect this woman I love. Please." His voice cracked on the last word.

Darcy never prayed aloud, certainly not when anybody could hear her. But words rose inside her, compelling her to speak. "Lord, thank You for this moment and this man. Protect him and MJ. I know how much You love them. Love us."

Those last two words resonated inside her.

God loved MJ and Logan. And He loved her.

Of course He did. How had she ever doubted that?

Her father might not love her, but her father wasn't God. And God wasn't her father. And it was stupid to doubt the Creator of the universe because her dad didn't care about her. He didn't even really know her. He'd never tried.

But God knew everything about her, and He loved and valued her. He thought Darcy was precious. "Protect me, Lord. You are able."

Logan's *amen* rumbled in her ear.

She took a breath. "It's time."

"I know." He kissed her forehead and released her.

She looked up through the opening as a cloud moved in front of the sun. The cavern darkened.

It wasn't a sign. Just a cloud. Hoping she hid her dread, she turned to Logan with a bright smile. "Give me a boost."

He didn't smile back. "Be safe."

"I'll do everything you said."

He paused only a moment before hoisting her up.

Squeezing between the rocks, she pushed herself outside, then turned and peeked back down. "See you soon."

Logan stared up through the gap, face grim. "Take care of yourself. I need you back."

Emotion clogged her throat. "Promise." The single word came out squeaky.

She had to go.

Protect me, Lord.

Staying low, she jogged away from the drop-off that marked the top of the cliff wall. Within a few minutes, she was deep in the forest, far from the cave, the cliff, and the man who was hunting her.

She was safe. Of course she was safe.

But the sun remained behind the clouds, the wind picked up, and nothing felt safe at all.

CHAPTER TWENTY-ONE

Logan checked his watch.

Darcy had been gone for ten minutes. Only ten. How far had she gotten?

His directions should take her to an old wildlife trail that led up from the pond, toward the rounded peak. This wasn't a steep mountain. She'd have a gentle climb.

But he had no idea if the path was still there. It'd been years since he'd seen it, but animals needed water, and the pond was the best source this high up.

Would Darcy find the trail? Would it be too overgrown for her to travel?

What if she got hurt? Injured? Mauled by a wildcat?

Calm down, Webb. He was going to give himself a heart attack.

How long would it take her to reach the retreat center? An hour? Maybe two? Would she run into searchers before then?

Logan sat in the shadow near the cave entrance, out of sight of Jonas.

MJ had moved deeper into the space when he returned, all false cheer gone.

"You think she's okay?"

It irritated him that she asked. If MJ had backed him up, Darcy would still be here, safe with them.

Except...were they safe?

"He's still here," Logan said. "She should be fine."

He kept his focus on the camo jacket. He couldn't see it now, but he'd studied him enough since they'd reached the cave. The man's size and shape matched what he remembered about Jonas. Unfortunately, he'd kept his face covered, so Logan couldn't confirm it.

Jonas shifted now and then but hadn't moved from his post behind the tree since Logan returned.

"When was the last time he checked the fire?" he asked.

"A few minutes ago."

The thin trail of smoke was gone. Whether because the wind carried it away or because Jonas had extinguished the fire, Logan didn't know.

The air had changed. This morning had been beautiful and clear, but clouds now darkened the sun, bringing wind and the scent of rain.

Let Darcy get to the retreat center before the skies open up, Lord.

Keep her safe.

As long as the guy stayed at the bottom of the cliff, Darcy would be safe.

But the stillness, the staring... It was getting to him.

He needed to *do* something.

He inched closer to the cave opening, risking being seen— and shot at. But he'd see the rifle before the man could take aim. Logan took a deep breath and shouted. "Hey!"

The man didn't move. Didn't even flinch.

"What are you doing?" MJ sounded horrified.

"Trying to distract him." He raised his voice again. "Jonas! It's your old friend Logan. Show yourself."

He waited, figuring the rifle would come into view.

But the camo jacket didn't move.

Fear niggled. Why didn't the shooter do *something*? If it was Jonas, surely he'd react to the fact that Logan knew his name.

"Come on, you coward," he shouted. "You can fire at two unarmed women"—his voice echoed—"but you're afraid to face me?"

Show yourself.

His fear grew and darkened like the clouds overhead.

A gust of wind bent the treetops and shimmied in the shrubs.

It lifted the arm of the jacket.

Which flapped like a flag.

No.

Logan stood, banged his head on the ceiling but ignored the pain. "He's not there!"

"What?" MJ crawled toward the opening.

"He's not there! The jacket..." Logan didn't have time to explain.

Where was Jonas?

Where was Darcy?

He couldn't think it through. He only knew Jonas—or whoever it was—had outsmarted him.

Think, Webb.

He yanked the handgun from his pocket and held it out. "Take it."

MJ did. "What are you—?"

"Stay here." He moved out of the cave and onto the steep slope.

MJ poked her head out. "Where are you going?"

"To find her." He was already climbing.

The fact that no gunshot sounded, no bullet ripped through his body, proved he was right. The gunman was gone.

He spoke over his shoulder. "Be vigilant. Shoot him if you have to."

"Wait!"

But there was no time to wait. A killer was out there, somewhere.

And so was Darcy.

CHAPTER TWENTY-TWO

Darcy wasn't exactly outdoorsy. Was indoorsy a thing? She'd left the cave and cliff behind, along with MJ and Logan and the man who'd been shooting at them.

Jonas?

Whoever it was, he was watching the mouth of the cave. She shouldn't be afraid. She'd been walking for ten minutes, holding the handgun. She was alone, nothing but little woodland creatures skittering among the leaves and bracken to keep her company. She prayed all the creatures she encountered would be little.

This was terrifying enough without running into a moose or a bear. Would she have the time to shoot if one charged her? Or the courage?

Breathe, Darcy.

There was no reason to be afraid.

Nothing was going to attack her. The biggest risk right now was getting lost.

Logan had told her to go to the eastern edge of the pond. He'd even clarified with a quick, *You know, the side nearest the sun.* Trying to be funny, despite the fear he hadn't quite masked in his expression.

But it was nearing noon, which would put the sun overhead. And even if it could direct her, it was hidden behind thick and dark clouds.

She made it to the pond and circled to the opposite side. Or at least she thought she was on the opposite side, but how would she know? The little body of water was surrounded by forest. Brown trunks, white trunks. Green bushes. Gray rocks.

Everything looked the same.

Which way was east?

Think, think.

Logan had told her once that moss grew on the north side of rocks. Seemed to her the squishy green plant grew all over everything. She examined a fallen log and... Ah, yes. The moss was concentrated on one side.

That must be north.

She faced that direction and imagined Canada straight ahead. So California was to her left.

To her right, she spotted a clump of white birch trees on what must be the easternmost edge of the pond and made her way to it, then searched for a path.

A very narrow strip of trodden grass led upward. Maybe that was the path Logan wanted her to follow. Maybe not.

Path or no path, Logan had told her to go up and east.

She stepped into the shadows among the trees, shivering in the wind.

The weather had shifted. The beauty she'd enjoyed at the pond's edge that morning was long gone. A chill filled the air, moist with the threat of rain.

No rain, please.

Now that she'd started praying again, she couldn't seem to

stop. If God was listening, why not talk to Him? Was He too busy with His divine tasks to listen? If so, she figured a God as powerful as the one Logan believed in could probably figure a way to tune her out. Her own father had certainly perfected that skill.

Nope.

She wasn't doing that anymore, comparing Dad with God. They weren't the same. Dad was distant and uncaring. God loved her. Back in high school, she'd read her Bible consistently. For a time, she'd highlighted all the verses that confirmed God's love, amazed at the sheer number of them. She remembered one now, something about how God had demonstrated His love because, while she was still sinning, He died for her.

Amazing. How had she let herself forget?

Ten years of living and working among nonbelievers had taken their toll. But her lack of faith couldn't be blamed on the people she spent time with. There were churches in Manhattan. She'd just never bothered to visit one.

She'd let her faith falter.

Not anymore.

God was with her. *Lord, keep me—*

A loud snap cut off the prayer.

She glanced to the right, registering movement an instant too late.

Black T-shirt. Black jeans. Black ski mask.

A scream crawled up her throat, choked off by panic.

She raised her pistol, but the man was already there. He grabbed her wrist and angled the weapon away.

With his other hand, he took it out of her hand.

Just like that.

She hadn't even thought to pull the trigger, which might've summoned help, if nothing else.

The man shifted behind her, wrapped an arm around her torso, and held her against his chest.

Cold metal pressed against her head.

She shrank away, trying to become as small as possible. To disappear.

She couldn't breathe. Couldn't think. Couldn't move.

"I don't want to hurt you," the man said. Then, angry, "Stay on your feet."

This man's voice was too deep, his accent definitely not Connecticut.

If it were Jonas, she might be able to talk her way out of this. But it wasn't Jonas.

Her legs were jelly. She wanted to collapse, to roll into a ball. To hide.

But it was too late to hide. He had her.

He had her!

"Listen to me." The gun lifted from her temple. "Listen to me."

She had to get away. She pushed at the arm wrapped around her middle, trying to free herself. Desperate to run.

He held on tighter. "Listen to me!" He sounded furious. "Stop fighting me or I'm going to hurt you."

Okay. Okay.

She didn't know what to do, but she wasn't strong enough to get away. She wasn't going to defeat him.

"Breathe," the man said. "Do it. In and out."

She obeyed. Breathing helped. The panic waned. Her brain caught up.

He'd found her. But he hadn't hurt her. Or killed her. Yet.

"I'm not here for you," the man said. "Say it. Say, 'You're not here for me.'"

"You're not here for me." Her voice sounded off, shaky and distant.

"You'll be safe if you do what I say. Say it."

"I'll be safe if I do what you say."

"Good, Darcy. Very good."

He knew her name. But how? Who was this?

"We're going to walk back to the pond," he said. "You're going to stay in front of me. You're not going to run. You're not going to fight. You understand? Say you understand."

"I understand."

"Don't make me hurt you. Okay?"

She nodded, but he said, "I need to hear it."

"I won't run." Her heart was racing. Every cell in her body trembled. She tried to swallow the terror that clogged her throat. "I won't fight you."

"That's all I ask." He turned her back toward the pond. "Let's go."

CHAPTER TWENTY-THREE

Logan hurried silently through the woods, staying near the edge of the water. He'd left MJ behind, despite her demands.

Wait!

I'm coming with you!

Don't you dare leave me here, Logan Webb!

He dared.

She'd be safer in the cave, and out here, she'd only slow him down.

He'd owe her a huge apology when this was over, but right now all he could think about was getting to Darcy before Jonas did.

Jonas had outsmarted him. The shame of it burned like acid. But where did he go?

To get something to force them out—or even to kill them while they were holed up in the cave? If that was the case, then Logan had left MJ to face the coming danger alone.

But what could Jonas possibly get? A grenade? A bomb? A bazooka?

There wasn't exactly a Munitions-Are-Us store in Shadow Cove.

Logan chewed on that as he jogged. He passed the boulder where he and MJ had hidden that morning—seemed like days before. He kept to the forest, avoiding anything that hinted of a trail. Because, much as he might like to think Jonas had left the mountain for supplies, he couldn't convince himself.

No. He was out here. Somewhere.

What if Logan was wrong about everything?

Maybe Jonas wasn't the shooter.

Maybe Darcy wasn't the target.

He stopped, catching his breath, and turned back toward the cave.

He'd given MJ his Ruger, and she knew how to shoot. She'd said so herself, hadn't she? But how many years since she'd pulled a trigger? How much experience did she have?

Should he go back and protect Darcy's aunt?

Definitely, Darcy would say.

Absolutely not, MJ would say.

The thought of leaving Darcy to fend for herself made him physically ill.

He couldn't do it.

He resumed his jog upward, staying parallel to where he'd sent Darcy, keeping his eyes and ears open. She should be ahead of him, but he was accustomed to traveling in the woods. He could move faster. He could catch up.

He had a feeling he needed to, soon. Because maybe it was Jonas out there, searching for Darcy.

Or maybe everything Logan had assumed about this shooter was wrong.

Maybe the man *did* know these woods. Logan had assumed the killer wasn't a local, as if his own friends and customers and neighbors couldn't be guilty of sending death threats, much less acting on them.

Stupid.

And if that was the case, then maybe the shooter had already known about the cave. And maybe he'd known there was another way out.

How, though? The gap had been filled in with dirt and debris. The only way the man could've known it was there was if he'd been there years before. Which was possible, of course. Logan and his dad weren't the only people who hunted these woods.

If the shooter had known, then maybe he'd anticipated that someone would get out through the gap in the cavern's ceiling. Maybe he'd been waiting...

Maybe Darcy was already dead.

No.

Logan hadn't heard a gunshot. He hadn't heard...anything.

He stopped again, breathing heavily, and scanned the area. Where was she?

Where was the shooter? Maybe he should go back—

"Daar-ceee!" MJ's call was faint but unmistakable.

What was she doing? If the killer was nearby, she was drawing him right to her!

And maybe...maybe that was the point. She believed the killer was after her. Maybe she thought that she could lure him away from her niece by putting herself in his crosshairs.

Logan turned and ran back down the slope, leaping rocks and skirting bushes. He had to get to MJ. Protect her. If nothing else, quiet her down.

But Darcy...

He wanted to find her. He was desperate to find the woman he loved.

Protect her, Lord. Please.

"Daar-ceee!"

Logan pushed himself faster, willing the older woman to shut up. To hide and be silent.

The woods were dark and deep, but up ahead, he saw a slight brightening. A clearing.

The pond.

He slowed at the sight of his father's yellow sweatshirt. MJ was in the woods but easy to pick out against the dark forest. She lifted her hands, cupped them at her mouth, and shouted, "Daar-ceee!"

Logan halted and waved his hands to get her attention.

Their eyes met, and he cut his finger across his neck in the universal sign for *knock it off*.

She raised her hands to yell again, ignoring him.

A gunshot blasted.

MJ fell.

No!

Logan fought the urge to run to her. Instead, he crouched, gaze scanning the opposite side of the pond. Even as close as he'd been, he wasn't sure where the shot had come from.

He turned back to where Darcy's aunt had fallen.

She wasn't there.

He peered into the brush surrounding the pond. Had he misjudged? Or...

No. She was moving, crawling deeper into the forest. Thank God.

Stay down!

The shooter was close, and Logan was unarmed. His only advantage was surprise.

MJ was alive, for now. Whether she'd been hit or not, he didn't know.

Where was Darcy?

Logan forced himself to pause and take stock. To look and listen.

All was still.

He scanned the forest around the lake again more slowly, searching for anything out of place.

And then movement caught his eye. There was something light gray against the black shadows.

Darcy's sweatshirt.

She was face down in the dirt.

Acid pooled in his stomach. *Please, please. Let her be alive.*

A masked man stood near her, partially hidden by a tree, aiming a rifle toward the pond. He wasn't tall, maybe five-eight or five-nine, and well-built.

It wasn't Jonas. Jonas was at least Logan's height, over six feet.

The man took a few steps nearer the water and shouted, "MJ Partington. Show yourself."

Logan whipped his gaze back to where he'd last seen MJ. *Don't do it. Stay hidden.*

"This is very simple, MJ." The shooter's voice sounded muffled—probably the fault of the ski mask.

It also sounded...familiar.

Logan shook his head to rid it of the crazy thought that invaded. It couldn't be.

"Your life for your niece's," the gunman yelled. "I don't blame Darcy. The consequences of your sins are for you to pay."

MJ had fallen at the gunshot, but obviously the shooter knew he'd missed.

Logan crept around the pond. His only chance was to take him by surprise.

And not get shot in the process.

"Here's the thing, MJ." The killer's voice was loud but somehow also conversational.

The more he spoke, the deeper Logan's sense of dread.

It couldn't be. He wouldn't believe it. Fear and fatigue were playing tricks on him. Had to be. Because that voice couldn't possibly belong to—

"Darcy didn't write the book that ruined lives," he shouted, "but she told people about it."

Logan had to get there, now. He couldn't think about what he'd do when he did.

He had no choice.

Help me, Father.

"She's the reason so many unsuspecting victims read it." The man's reasoned tone belied the fury that must lie beneath. "I don't want to hurt her, but if I have to settle for killing the person who brought that book into my daughter's life, I will."

No, no, no.

Please!

The brush was thick between Logan and the shooter. If he went straight through, he'd make too much noise.

He crept deeper into the forest, where a blanket of pine needles cushioned his footsteps.

"I'm getting tired of waiting."

Logan was twenty feet away. Eighteen.

"Are you really going to let your niece die for you?"

Fifteen.

"You have to the count of three. One!"

Logan stepped around a pile of dead brush.

Two!"

Ten feet, but the man stood on the far side of a thick thorn bush. Logan shifted to go around it.

Darcy came into view, lying at the gunman's feet. Her arms were over her head protectively, as if that might help.

But the posture meant she was alive.

"That's it." The killer pointed the rifle at Darcy's head.

"I'm here!" MJ shouted. "Don't shoot her. I'm here!"

The killer aimed his weapon toward the defenseless woman on the far side of the pond.

"No!" Logan screamed and charged.

The rifle swung toward him.

The gun exploded.

Far away, a woman screamed.

CHAPTER TWENTY-FOUR

I t happened so fast.

Darcy had known MJ would show herself. She wouldn't risk Darcy's life.

What had she been thinking, shouting like that?

Trying to draw the man away from Darcy and back to her, obviously.

Even so, her aunt's voice carrying over the pond had been the most terrible sound she'd ever heard.

The killer had forced Darcy to walk toward the noise, one hand over her mouth to keep her from shouting a warning. The other holding the handgun to her head. They'd reached the clearing, and he'd lifted the pistol from her head and aimed across the pond.

Darcy hadn't been thinking.

She'd shoved herself against him. The shot went wild.

She shouldn't have been surprised at his furious backhand. Or the way he'd forced her onto the ground, facedown. That telltale click rifles made ticked up her terror.

She dared not move while this man tried to bargain, a life for a life.

MJ's *I'm here* hadn't surprised Darcy at all.

Logan's shout, however, had shocked her even as she flipped over and kicked the shooter's kneecap.

The gun went off.

Logan tackled the guy, and they landed in the dirt beside her.

The rifle flew a few feet away.

Darcy scrambled to it. She aimed it, but she couldn't shoot the guy, not with Logan so close.

Logan had already subdued him. He kneeled over him but wasn't fighting. It was more like he was avoiding the man's wild punches.

Not hitting back.

"Stop it!" Logan shouted. "It's me. Stop fighting!"

What in the...?

The man reached for his pocket, where he'd stowed her handgun.

"Logan, watch out!"

CHAPTER TWENTY-FIVE

Logan couldn't process it. Or maybe he didn't want to as the man yanked a gun from his pocket.

Logan slammed his fist into the black mask, then shifted to kneel on the killer's wrist.

Not a killer. He hadn't done it.

But he would have.

A truth Logan couldn't process right now. Maybe ever.

"Stop moving or I'm really gonna hurt you."

The shooter lay still, breathing heavily, but Logan didn't trust it. He stared down at those familiar brown eyes. "Do you really want to shoot me?"

He blinked but said nothing, as if he could hide his identity behind a mask and silence.

It was too late for that.

Logan grabbed the handgun and held it out behind him. "You okay, Darcy?"

She took it but didn't speak.

He glanced back and saw a line of blood dripping from her head. The sight of it filled him with fury.

His fingers itched to stretch around this man's neck and

squeeze. He leaned close and whispered, "What did you do to her?"

Again, no answer.

"You tried to kill the woman I love. How could you?"

In the distance, an engine growled.

Logan didn't look at Darcy but straightened his back. "Fire a bullet in the air so whoever that is knows where we are. I'm guessing they're looking for us."

A boom erupted.

The man beneath him flinched.

Logan glared down at him. "Did you think you were going to get away with it? Did you think I wouldn't figure it out?"

"Logan?" Darcy's voice held confusion, but he didn't know how to explain.

Nothing could explain this.

The man's eyes filled with tears. He blinked, and a few escaped and seeped into the fabric of the mask.

Darcy crawled near, stopping a few feet away but in his line of sight. "Logan? What's going on?"

She was so beautiful, so gentle. So vulnerable.

And this man...this man he'd loved...

"Do you know him?" she asked.

Logan couldn't seem to make his voice work. He yanked off the mask and revealed the face of someone he'd known all his life. His spiritual mentor. His late father's best friend.

"It's Miles."

CHAPTER TWENTY-SIX

W hoa.

What?

Darcy had never seen such heartbreak in Logan's eyes. Even at the funeral, he hadn't looked like he did now. His father's death had been a tragic accident.

But this man's actions had been cold, calculated, and cruel.

MJ stumbled through the bushes and collapsed at Darcy's side, pulling her into a hug.

"Oh, sweetheart. Are you all right? I was so worried."

Darcy hugged her aunt back. Thank God she was alive. She leaned away and took in her beloved face, each beautiful wrinkle, those terrified and tear-filled eyes.

"You're bleeding." MJ swiped at Darcy's temple, then shrugged out of the sweatshirt, exposing the camisole she'd worn beneath her jacket the day before. She pressed the fabric to the wound.

Darcy hadn't even felt the pain until that moment. It was nothing compared to what could've happened.

"It's your fault my Linny is dead." Miles's words were cold. "Her husband left her because of you."

MJ leaned away, even though Logan hadn't let up his hold on the gunman. Her eyes were wide with shock and confusion.

"Stop talking." Logan's tone held a threat.

But Miles either didn't hear it or didn't care. "My grandchild died because of you."

"I said shut up." Logan pressed his hand over the older man's mouth, but Miles whipped his head to the side.

"She killed herself because of you."

Logan covered the man's mouth again, and this time, he didn't let the gunman squirm away. "Linny had a miscarriage. She was an addict who relapsed. None of that was MJ's fault."

The engine noises were getting louder, coming from higher on the mountain.

And then a gray-haired cop stepped out of the forest.

His gun was drawn. He focused first on Darcy. "Drop it."

"Oh." She'd forgotten she held the handgun. She did, then pushed it away from her.

He turned to Logan. "What's going on, son?"

Logan backed away and stood. "He tried to kill us."

"Not you." The man's voice, so hard a moment before, held only defeat now. Sorrow and heartbreak. "That's why I didn't shoot her this morning. I couldn't risk hitting you."

The cop's eyebrows hiked, but he said nothing. Smart man to let the would-be killer confess.

"You're like a son to me." Miles's voice held genuine grief. "I would never have hurt you."

"You already did. You almost killed the woman I love." He circled to where Darcy still sat, pulled her to her feet, and crushed her to his chest.

While the cop read Miles his rights and cuffed him, while other police officers streamed in, Darcy held onto Logan.

She would never let him go again.

CHAPTER TWENTY-SEVEN

B ack at the retreat center, Logan sat on one of the sofas that lined the banquet room, elbows on his knees, head in his hands, still trying to process what had happened.

Miles.

The man who'd coached him when he'd taken over Dad's business, who'd encouraged him as he'd tried to guide his siblings, who'd mentored him in his relationship with Christ...

The man who'd become a surrogate father to him after Dad's death...

Had attempted murder.

Logan didn't understand.

He'd been questioned by police and then told he could go home. But he wasn't leaving until he saw Darcy and MJ, who'd been questioned and then given a room upstairs to get cleaned up.

The common area was packed with people, cops and locals who'd been searching. They were sipping from water bottles, snacking on the tray of food somebody had brought, and chatting about the day's events. This was the most exciting thing to happen in Shadow Cove since...Logan couldn't even remember.

He resented the festive atmosphere.

Logan's mom was seated in a chair nearby. She and his siblings had been waiting, worried, when Logan, Darcy, and MJ arrived with the police. Once they knew he was all right, Jewel, Laine, and Ryder had gone to the restaurant, which they hadn't opened that morning.

It was tempting to worry about the revenue they'd lost, but Logan refused to allow it. God had protected them, all of them. Even Miles hadn't been hurt.

A God who could do that could handle a little lost income.

Logan had given his mom the short version of events from the front porch while they'd watched as Miles was transferred, handcuffed, from a four-wheeler to the back of a police car.

Miles hadn't just betrayed Logan. He'd betrayed Mom. He'd betrayed Dad.

Mom had regained her voice after the police car rolled away. "He's not in his right mind. Grief can do crazy things to a person."

Logan didn't want anyone making excuses for Miles. How many times had he told Logan to take every thought captive? Apparently, he was a *do as I say, not as I do* kind of guy. He'd definitely let some pretty evil thoughts not only enter his mind, but take root and spread.

Now, sitting on the sofa, Logan asked himself... How much pain must Miles have been in since Linny died?

How had Logan missed it?

He'd be asking himself that question for a long time.

A shadow crossed over him, and something plopped on the coffee table in front of him.

"You all right?" The voice wasn't familiar.

The owner of the retreat center, Sam Wright, looked down at Logan. He was a few years older than Logan, a few inches over six feet. Dark hair, trimmed beard. His eyes were filled with concern.

"I'm okay." Logan started to stand.

"Don't get up, man. You're good."

Logan turned to introduce him to his mother, but she wasn't there.

Sam settled in the club chair adjacent to the couch. "I thought you might be hungry." He nodded to a sack from a local deli.

Logan's stomach growled. "I bet Darcy and MJ could use—"

"Your mom took a couple of sandwiches up. What else do you need?"

"Nothing. I'm..." Not fine. He wasn't sure how to finish the sentence.

"Miles," Sam said. "It's shocking. Do you know what happened?"

"His daughter was a drug addict. She went to rehab a few years ago and got clean. She got married and seemed to be doing all right—as far as I knew, anyway. About eighteen months ago, her husband left her. She relapsed. I'm not sure if she knew she was pregnant when she started using again, but she lost the baby. And then she overdosed. By the time Miles found her, it was too late."

Sam nodded slowly, taking that in. "I don't understand what that has to do with... He was trying to kill the author who was here, right?"

"MJ Partington, yeah. He blamed her. I'm guessing his son-in-law read her book. Maybe that's why he left Linny." Though, really, the man had to have been considering it already. It would take a lot more than a couple of lines in a self-help book to get someone to throw away his marriage vows.

"You knew her?" Sam asked. "Linny?"

"When we were kids. She was just a nice, normal girl, you know?"

"Drugs."

"Yeah."

Mom settled on the sofa beside him. He waited for her to tell him to eat, but she didn't. Instead, she engaged Sam in conversation.

Logan was thankful. Not that he didn't appreciate the food, but he didn't have it in him to talk. He just wanted to see Darcy.

He opened the sack and ate. Hungry as he was, he should've savored the sandwich, but he barely tasted it, keeping his gaze on the staircase.

Finally, Darcy came down the stairs. Her hair was wet, her face freshly scrubbed. A bandage covered the cut on her fore-head, but otherwise she looked perfect in a T-shirt, too-long jeans rolled up at the ankles, and flip-flops. He had no idea where the clothes had come from. She reminded him of the casual girl she used to be as she stopped on the landing halfway down and scanned the crowd.

Logan plopped the rest of his sandwich on the coffee table and stood, catching her eye.

Her shoulders visibly relaxed.

He felt the same way.

He scooted past Mom and the throng of locals who'd spent their morning searching. He was thankful for them, but at the moment, all he wanted was Darcy, who was descending the stairs toward him.

When they reached each other, he opened his arms, and she stepped in.

The murmur of voices faded until all that mattered was the woman in his arms. She smelled of soap and shampoo. He wished he'd showered, not wanting to contaminate her with his stench.

But Darcy didn't seem to mind as she held onto him, her cheek pressed against his sweatshirt.

They stood like that for a long moment, just holding each other.

She looked up at him, her eyes filled with tears. "Are you all right?"

"Are you?" When she nodded, he said, "Then I am too. How's MJ?"

"She took a shower and then crawled into bed. I don't think we can stay here, but neither one of us is ready to get on a plane."

The words were a punch to the gut. Of course she had to return to New York.

He stepped back but took her hand. "Come on." He led the way up the stairs, past the second floor to the third. Miles had given him a grand tour of the retreat center a few days before. He didn't have a lot of appreciative feelings toward his former mentor at the moment, but he was thankful for this.

They walked down a hall and through an empty lounge space, and then Logan pushed open a door onto a balcony that spanned the rear of the property.

He stepped aside, and Darcy gasped. "It's beautiful."

Logan followed her gaze past the wide yard used for weddings and other events to the forest that sloped down the mountain. In the distance, the little village of Shadow Cove hugged the rugged Atlantic. The clouds that'd moved in earlier had blown past and now hovered on the eastern horizon, leaving mostly sunshine behind.

He leaned a hip against the railing and faced Darcy. "I hoped we could talk."

Her expression was so open and trusting, as if there was nothing he could say that she wouldn't want to hear. But he wasn't the one about to break a heart in this conversation.

He didn't even know how to start. But, when it came right down to it, what he wanted to say was simple. "I love you."

She smiled. "I love you."

"But my life is here, and even if I wanted to move—"

She shut him up with a finger over his mouth. "As awful and scary as this has been, Logan, I realized something in the last twenty-four hours. I've been chasing the wrong dream. I've spent my whole life trying to impress my father, a man who doesn't even really know me."

Logan couldn't imagine. What a fool Partington was to miss out on someone as special as Darcy.

"I went to NYU to impress him. I went into publishing to impress him. I live in Manhattan to impress him. My whole life, I've just tried to live up to his standards—and failed."

"His standards are stupid," Logan said.

Darcy grinned. "You're right. And I'm done with all of that. I realized something today. I have a Father, and He loves me, whether my earthly dad does or not. And I realized something else, something I've refused to admit for a decade. Longer than that, really. Probably since I was a kid. Dad thought he was too good for Maine. He used to talk about how he brushed the dust of Maine off his shoes and moved on to bigger and better. Well, New York might be bigger, but better?" She shook her head. "Not for me. Shadow Cove is where I belong. I was never happier than when I was here. I was never happier than when I was with you."

"Really?" Logan's heart, already full, felt like it could burst. "You'd really move here?"

"I'll have to give my notice and break my lease, but if you want me, then—"

"Yes. Please." He chuckled, trying to find a way to express just how much he wanted her. But there were no words.

Instead, he took her in his arms and covered her mouth with

his. She tasted of toothpaste and promise, and he wanted more of her. All of her. But he forced himself to move softly, gently. This didn't have to be the kiss to end all kisses.

Instead, it was just the beginning.

He leaned away but didn't let her go.

She smiled up at him, tears shining in her eyes. "Wow."

Wow, indeed. "In case you weren't sure, I want you." He held her close and whispered in her ear. "Forever."

The End.

~

...for now, but you don't want to miss the *Escaping with You Bonus Epilogue*. Download it for free at subscribepage.io/escaping_with _you.

You got a glimpse of Sam Wright in this story. **You're not going to believe what happens to him next.** It all starts when the only woman Sam ever loved shows up on his doorstep and throws herself into his arms—as if she never left him. As if she has no memory of the past five years.

She has amnesia—and a bunch of bruises she can't explain. And it just gets twistier from there. Don't miss *Running to You*, book one in the Wright Heroes of Maine series. Turn the page for more about *Running to You*.

Sam never understood why Eliza left him five years ago, ghosting him without explanation. He's avoided romance ever since, focusing on building his business. Money might not keep him warm at night, but it can sure buy a lot of blankets.

Then Eliza shows up on his doorstep and throws herself into his arms. She can't explain her bruises or the head injury that's left her with no memories of the past five years, including their breakup. No matter how good it feels to hold her, though, there's no way he's getting sucked into romance again.

He'll deliver Eliza to her mother, and that will be that. But instead of finding her mom, they're met by two attackers and barely escape alive. Despite the danger to his life and his heart, he can't leave Eliza to fend for herself.

Together, they embark on a journey to reconstruct her past while evading the men chasing her. As Sam and Eliza close in on the truth, their romance reignites, but her secret threatens to destroy them both.

Prepare to be enthralled by this gripping story of amnesia, a second chance at love, and a secret baby. *Running to You* is an edge-of-your-seat Christian romantic suspense set in Maine that will keep you reading all night long.

Inheritance of Secrets

Lineage of Corruption

Wreathed in Disgrace

Courage in the Shadows

Vengeance in the Mist

A Mountain Too Steep

The Nutfield Saga

Convenient Lies

Twisted Lies

Generous Lies

Innocent Lies

Beautiful Lies

Legacy Rejected

Legacy Restored

Legacy Reclaimed

Legacy Redeemed

Sleigh Bells & Stalkers

One Christmas Night

Amanda Series

Chasing Amanda

Finding Amanda

ABOUT ROBIN PATCHEN

Robin Patchen is a *USA Today* bestselling and award-winning author of Christian romantic suspense. She grew up in a small town in New Hampshire, the setting of her Coventry Saga books, and then headed to Boston to earn a journalism degree. After college, working in marketing and public relations, she discovered how much she loathed the nine-to-five ball and chain. She started writing her first novel while she home-schooled her three children. The novel was dreadful, but her passion for storytelling didn't wane. Thankfully, as her children grew, so did her skill. Now that her kids are adults, she has more time to play with the lives of fictional heroes and heroines, wreaking havoc and working magic to give her characters happy endings. When she's not writing, she's editing or reading, proving that most of her life revolves around the twenty-six letters of the alphabet.

Learn more about Robin Patchen: http://robinpatchen.com